CLAIMING THE ALPHA

ALSO BY ALICIA MONTGOMERY

The True Mates Series

Fated Mates

Blood Moon

Romancing the Alpha

Witch's Mate

Taming the Beast

Tempted by the Wolf

The Lone Wolf Defenders Series

Killian's Secret

Loving Quinn

All for Connor

The True Mates Standalone Novels

Holly Jolly Lycan Christmas

A Mate for Jackson: Bad Alpha Dads

True Mates Generations

A Twist of Fate

Claiming the Alpha

Alpha Ascending

A Witch in Time

Highland Wolf

Daughter of the Dragon

Shadow Wolf

A Touch of Magic

The Blackstone Mountain Series

The Blackstone Dragon Heir

The Blackstone Bad Dragon

The Blackstone Bear

The Blackstone Wolf

The Blackstone Lion

The Blackstone She-Wolf

The Blackstone She-Bear

The Blackstone She-Dragon

Edited by LaVerne Clark
Cover by Jacqueline Sweet

CLAIMING THE ALPHA

TRUE MATES GENERATIONS BOOK 2

ALICIA MONTGOMERY

PROLOGUE

Darius Corvinus surveyed the glitz and glamour of his surroundings, barely able to hide the contempt seething inside him. This gathering brought together some of the most prominent Lycans in the world, and to say that he felt out of place was an understatement.

The silk tuxedo tie around his neck felt like a noose, and he had to fight his every instinct to tug at it so he could breathe. His uncle Anatoli said it was necessary; that they would never let him into the ballroom of the Waldorf Astoria if he wasn't dressed properly. The gold-embossed invite on the cream linen paper wasn't enough to grant him entrance to the ascension ceremony of the two most powerful would-be Alphas in the world. He had to *look* like he belonged.

He huffed. Where did he belong? That was the question. Maybe it was far away, in that poor, dusty village in

Romania where he grew up. But it had been more than two decades since he'd been there, and he doubted he would even recognize it now much less feel at home there. But then again, he didn't feel like he belonged in America either. Not since—

Someone jostled him, knocking him out of his thoughts. He gritted his teeth, scoffing mentally at the people around him laughing and chatting without a care in the world. All these Lycans in such an enclosed space wasn't good for him, or his wild wolf. But relentless practice over the years had taught him to rein in his animal's nature. So that he could be normal. Or at least, appear to be anyway.

Being chosen to attend such a gathering should have been an honor. But his uncle Anatoli knew he would hate it. Perhaps that was the reason why he sent him here. As head of The Family, Anatoli Corvinus had every right to give him orders, and as his nephew and one of his enforcers, Darius had no choice but to obey. Privately, he had voiced his objections to Anatoli.

"Why must I go?" he had asked him. "Surely *you* must be the one to represent us."

"And that is the reason why I cannot be there," Anatoli answered. "I am far too busy with business for such trivial matters."

Darius bit his tongue, not wanting to point out that the ascension of a new Alpha—technically, *their* Alpha—was not a trivial matter. But then again, Frankie Anderson had all but abandoned her post as New Jersey's Alpha, so why should it matter who would be taking up the mantle after her? The Family could run their business as they had done the past few decades, no matter who the Alpha was.

"Champagne, sir?"

He stared down at the young woman holding up a tray of delicate glass flutes filled with bubbly liquid. *Human.* For a moment, her eyes widened in surprise and her mouth gaped. He was used to such a reaction, from both Lycans and non-Lycans alike. Usually it was the tattoos that covered most of his upper body that made people gawk, though his tuxedo jacket and shirt hid most of the ink on his skin. So, most likely, it was the shock of pure silvery gray hair on his head. If it wasn't for his height or bulk, most people would have thought he was an old man. The few who dared talk to him would often ask if he dyed his hair, to which he would just answer a simple *no*.

"Sir?" the young woman repeated.

He shook his head. "No, thank you."

She gave him a nod and walked away, proffering her drinks to the other guests. Alcohol was not something he enjoyed, and this certainly was not a celebration for him or The Family. Though he came as a representative, this was also part of business. When it came to The Family, everything was about the business. He was here to scope out the new Alpha, and to report any findings back to his uncle.

Something soft brushed past him, and he heard the rustle of fabric and felt the caress of silk against the back of his hand. He froze, his spine going all stiff. His inner wolf, too, went very still, its ears standing at attention. When he turned, he scented it—something sweet and delicious. He closed his eyes to get a better read on the scent. It reminded him of the sweet cheese pastries of his childhood, the ones his *bunică*—grandmother—used to make.

Slowly, he opened his eyes, his gaze fixing on the woman in a long dress walking away from him. He didn't know why, but he had an urge to follow her. And so he found himself weaving through the crowd, trailing after her delicious scent.

When she stopped to talk to a tall, blond man, he hung back so neither would notice him. His wolf growled at how the man seemed too familiar with her. He stood close—too close—as he spoke.

Why was he reacting this way? He had yet to see her face. Sure, he could tell she had generous curves from the way her sea-colored gown clung to her body, but he didn't even know what she looked like. Her hair though, looked silky and thick, and he wondered how it would feel between his fingers.

Soon the man left her alone. *Good.* Still, he couldn't bring himself to approach her or even overtake her so he could glimpse her face. Like he was almost afraid of what he'd see.

He kept a good distance between them, not too far that he lost sight of her, but not too close that anyone would notice. The moment he walked into the ballroom, he knew that the entire place was being watched carefully, most likely by the New York clan's famed Lycan security guards. Already, he counted them around the area—one in the far corner, a second in the mezzanine, and a third pretending to sip champagne as he spoke into a communication device tucked in his ear. It was not that they were terrible at blending in, but Darius was trained to see such things. And after a few minutes, he knew that they were watching *her* too.

Who was this mysterious woman?

She stopped and then pivoted on her heel, and if he had been less careful, she would have bumped straight into him. He quickly sidestepped so she wouldn't notice him, grabbing a champagne flute from a passing waiter's tray. Had he been faster, he would have seen her face, maybe even discovered what the color of her eyes were. When he finally reoriented himself and looked toward the direction where she ran off, she was gone.

He cursed, craning his neck for any sign of her. Her dress was distinct enough, but there were too many people. Surely she couldn't have gone too far. It would be easy enough to—

The explosion came unexpectedly, disorienting him. He thought it was a trick or that he was imagining it, but the ringing in his ears told him it was real. Before he could figure out what was happening, a second, even stronger explosion blasted into the room, knocking down several guests, including himself. He braced himself as his knees hit the floor, his palms smacking down on the hardwood, the only thing keeping him from sprawling over.

A growl ripped from his throat as he composed himself. He shot to his feet and assessed his environment.

Chaos reigned as people scrambled and ran for cover. Strange men dressed in robes entered through two giant gaping holes in the walls. Behind them, people in dark combat gear filed in, weapons raised and pointed into the throng of well-dressed guests.

His wolf coiled inside him, ready to pounce, to fight and to kill if necessary. His first thought, however, was the woman in the blue-green dress. Where was she? Had she made it out before the explosion?

His brain told him to leave now. This wasn't their fight. He needed to get out. *Stay alive.* He wasn't going to be collateral damage in some unknown war.

But his wolf was already fighting his brain, and he found himself heading straight into the thick of it all.

A cry made him turn his head. He'd never heard her speak but he just *knew*. That was her.

He turned toward the sound, his legs pumping as he sped across the ballroom. What he saw had his vision turning red. Two men dressed in robes standing over a figure slumped on the floor, a pool of silky blue-green fabric around their feet.

His wolf ripped out of him so fast that he felt light-headed. His animal leapt up and soared toward the two men. Its large paw reached out and swatted one man, knocking him down as the wolf sailed forward, opening its jaw as razor-sharp teeth went right for the other man's jugular. The wolf's mouth was so large it practically engulfed the man's head, and as it bore down, the satisfying crunch of bone filled his ears just as he felt the warm blood gushing into his mouth.

It didn't even take five seconds to take down both men. The wolf released what was left of its victim and turned to the unconscious woman on the floor.

Need to get her to safety.

The wolf wholeheartedly agreed with him for once and relinquished their body to him. He didn't waste a second and scooped her up into his arms, then made his way toward the exit, not really caring where he was going or that his clothes had ripped away in his hasty shift. All that mattered was to get her far away from those seeking to harm her.

He followed the rest of the people fleeing, down a long, carpeted hallway, but instead of heading into the lobby, he turned down another smaller hallway and into the first door he found—the ladies' restroom. He rushed into the plush sitting room and gently laid her down on the couch. Unable to stop himself, he pushed the strands of thick dark curls away from her face.

His chest tightened as he looked at the exquisite face of the woman who had captivated him and his wolf. He couldn't turn away and his gaze swept over her, starting from her delicately arched thick brows, her pert nose, and her plump lips. The dress she wore exposed her shoulders and the expanse of smooth olive skin of the tops of her lush breasts. He knew he shouldn't be admiring the assets of an unconscious woman, but he couldn't help himself. This was the body of a real woman, all curves and dips. Sturdy and well-built, made to be handled.

A soft gasp made him freeze. Her lips parted though she didn't move at all. When her eyes began to flutter, he held his breath. Though clouded and unfocused, he finally saw the color of her eyes. Rather, the colors. One blue and the other green. The color of the sky and the sea, a contrast that seemed to make her even more beguiling.

For a moment, they seemed to focus. They stared up at him, but her eyelids struggled to stay open before shutting again. He reached out to touch her cheek and felt a zing across his fingertips at the contact.

Who are you?

His inner wolf howled. The urge to take her away and protect her came over him. *A silly notion.* She was a stranger. Vulnerable, yes, but he didn't even know who she was.

He heard shuffling outside and went still. And he realized that it was unusually quiet. The chaos had died down. Perhaps the attackers had been defeated.

I'm a damn fool. He should have run at the first sign of danger. Who cares if all those Lycans had been killed? It would have been a boon to The Family as they would be able to go about their business without interference.

The doorknob creaked as it turned and he quickly dashed into one of the empty stalls, carefully closing the door and bracing himself against it. He closed his eyes, focusing his keen hearing on what was happening outside. Rustling fabric. The click-clack of heels on marble.

"Oh, God. What was I thinking?" There was a barely contained sob and a deep breath. "I shouldn't have told him—Adrianna?"

Adrianna? Why did that name sound familiar?

"Adrianna. Adrianna. It's me, Deedee. Wake up!" There was a sniff and a pause. "Oh, no. The mages must have hit you good with whatever potions they had. They're gone now, but ... don't worry, I'll get help and come back right away." He heard more movement and the sound of the door creaking open before it slammed shut.

Darius counted to ten before he carefully made his way out of the stall. The other woman said she would be back soon which meant he didn't have any time. He glanced back at the woman on the couch.

Adrianna.

As in, Adrianna *Anderson.* He recognized the name from the invitation. This was the New Jersey clan's soon-to-be Alpha. *His* Alpha.

It couldn't be. But surely there weren't many Adriannas here tonight. He was torn. His wolf refused to leave her side, but he knew that he couldn't be discovered here. There was too much at stake.

We must go, he told his wolf. He leashed it tight, ignoring its howling protests. The coast was clear outside, and it was now or never. Of course, there was the fact that he was fully naked, his shift having torn his tux and his car keys away. That only made his escape now more urgent. The trip back to New Jersey would be long, and it would have to be made in wolf form, but he had no choice.

And speaking of going back to The Family headquarters, there was the matter of what he would report back to Anatoli.

Worry about it later. For now, he had to go before anyone saw him.

CHAPTER ONE

Adrianna Anderson smiled to herself as she watched the bride and groom dance under the fairy lights, then let out a sigh. It was incredibly romantic, and she was happy that Astrid and Zac were lucky enough to find love in each other.

The wedding venue was a glass conservatory on a Brooklyn rooftop, so while the snow continued to fall outside, it was warm and toasty inside. The whole place looked magnificent, but the wedding couple didn't seem to notice their surroundings as they had eyes only for each other. The bride was practically glowing as her groom twirled her around and then pulled her back to him.

"Beautiful wedding, isn't it?"

"It definitely is." Adrianna turned around. "Nice to see you, sis. Been busy?"

Julianna Anderson smirked at her. "You know I'm

always busy." She crossed her arms over chest. "But I had to see this for myself."

"I think you're a cynic."

"You *know* I am," Julianna snorted.

Adrianna chuckled. Her middle sister was always so serious. Even now, dressed in a sleek gray pantsuit, her chin-length bob slicked back, she looked more like she was attending a funeral rather than a wedding. Working for the Lycan Security Force in the Special Investigations department was the perfect fit for her nature and personality. Her eyes—one blue and one green, as she shared the same heterochromia all the Anderson siblings had—showed a hardness that was way beyond her years.

"You don't believe in love? And True Mates? Even though our own parents were True Mates?"

"It's not that I don't believe in True Mates," Julianna said. "But I'm a realist."

"I think it's romantic." She had, after all, seen the attraction and love blossom between Astrid and Zac, and she liked to think she had somewhat of a hand in their getting together. "It's hard to believe they're the first True Mate pairing that's come out in the past couple of years."

"If I didn't see Astrid survive being burned to a crisp when the mages attacked us at the Waldorf, I wouldn't have believed it." Women who were pregnant with their mate's child were invulnerable, one of the few signs of a real True Mate pairing. "Too bad you missed it, since you were passed out in the bathroom."

Adrianna stiffened at the mention of the failed ascension ceremony. They had nearly lost their lives when their enemies, the mages, had attacked. Her inner she-wolf, the animal she shared her body with, bristled with anger. It had wanted to attack, to protect them from the mages, but they had hit her with a confounding potion that knocked her out before she could even shift. Apparently, she and her twin, Lucas, were their main targets.

They told her she had been found in the ladies' room at the Waldorf Astoria after the attack. She couldn't remember how she got there, but since then, she'd been plagued by dreams of that night. A shiver ran down her spine.

Every night for the past two weeks, she would go to sleep, waiting for the dreams to come. She was sure they did, but as soon as she woke up, they seemed to fade away leaving only small bits like pieces of a jigsaw puzzle coming together to form one picture. A flash of silver. Dark whorls of ink over muscled, taut skin. The image of a bird. A delicious vanilla scent. And last night, it was cobalt blue eyes staring back at her with a heat that made her skin burn.

Her wolf whined at the memory. Whined with what? It felt like a deep-seated need, a longing she couldn't place. Her wolf, normally pleasant and placated, had been antsy since for some reason. It was restless and clawed at her, begging to be let out. She snorted at the thought. Let out in the middle of the city? *No way.* Lycans weren't allowed to shift around humans. It was too risky.

"Hello, earth to Adrianna?"

Julianna waved a hand in front of her face and she snapped out of the trance. "Yes?"

"Jeez, you're such a head case. Are you okay?"

"Yeah, I'm fine. Have you seen Lucas?" she asked, changing the subject.

"He's fine," Julianna replied. "I'm sorry. I didn't realize how this must be affecting you two, being twins and all."

The attack at the ascension ball wasn't the first time the mages had struck. It was actually the second, which was why their parents decided it would be best if she and Lucas weren't in the same place at the same time. At first, it seemed easy enough. It's not like she and her brother were joined at the hip, but to actively avoid each other was different. Sure, they could always call and message each other, but it was different not being able to just have dinner or lunch together, or even to ride in the same car to work. He'd even had to move out of The Enclave and was staying at one of the brownstones their family owned on the Upper West Side.

"I miss him." It had been a tough choice between who would attend the wedding tonight as Zac had been a close friend to both of them growing up. Lucas deferred to his sister, and Zac understood the situation.

"I know. He misses you too," Julianna said in a somber voice. "But I came over here because Mama wants to talk to you about something important."

Adrianna bristled. "*Now?*"

Her sister shrugged. "Hey, I'm just the messenger. Let's go, before she comes over here and drags us away."

"Right."

While she followed Julianna as they weaved their way across the reception area, Adrianna couldn't help but feel like someone was watching her. She turned her head but didn't see anyone in particular looking her way. She shrugged it off and continued to make her way toward her mother. Francesca "Frankie" Anderson was talking to a group of guests, but when she spied her daughters, quickly excused herself from the conversation.

"Come with me," she said, leading them away from the main reception area. They walked out of the conservatory and into the main building where Frankie ushered them into a small room. "The manager was nice enough to lend me her office so we could have some privacy."

"We really couldn't have talked at work?" Adrianna tried not to sound too annoyed. "Or at The Enclave? You know I'm only in the next building over."

"It's not like I haven't been trying to get ahold of you, Adrianna," Frankie retorted. "You seem to be having trouble returning my messages and calls lately."

"I've been busy," she said defensively.

Frankie sighed. "Look, let's not beat around the bush. You know this has been coming for a long time. Ascension ceremony aside, you must take your place as Alpha of New Jersey. Which means you need to actually *live* there. It's your duty. Your right."

She bit her tongue, not wanting to say what was really on her mind. The truth that would hurt Frankie so much. That she just didn't *want* the position and was perfectly fine with her life. Her job as President of Muccino International was fulfilling, and she loved managing their worldwide chain of restaurants. Her life was here in New York, *not* in New Jersey.

Unfortunately, she came from a long line of female Alphas or Lupas. The New Jersey clan was matriarchal, one of the few in the world. Her mother was Lupa in her own right, as was her mother before her, and her mother before that. Being Frankie's oldest daughter, she was next in line, and her mother's impending retirement meant she would be Alpha sooner rather than later.

"You've ruled as Alpha from New York for most of your life," Adrianna pointed out. "Why can't we keep doing the same thing? The open border policy between the two territories has always worked."

Lycan territories were clearly delineated, and members of one clan couldn't simply cross over to the other unless they had express permission. But, since Grant Anderson, Alpha of New York, and Frankie Muccino, Alpha of New Jersey, were married over thirty years ago, they had declared that New York and New Jersey Lycans could freely travel back and forth between the two territories.

"It *used* to work," Frankie said. "But we can't take chances. Not anymore."

"Why not?" Adrianna felt that famous Italian temper rise in her. She was still her mother's daughter after all. "Why can't I just rule from here? Or why do you even want to retire? Just because Papa is giving up his position as Alpha doesn't mean you have to as well."

Frankie let out a deep breath. "You don't understand. Things are different now. Especially with the threat of the mages. We can't let them win."

Her mother's voice faltered and for a moment, she saw something she'd never witnessed—her strong, tough-as-nails mother looked truly distressed. She had every right to be, of course; the mages, their mortal enemies, had nearly wiped them out back in the day. The Lycans fought and won, but they'd still lost many good people.

She reached over to take Frankie's hand in hers. "We won't let them, Mama." Sucking in a deep breath, she let the air fill her lungs, then blew out the breath to release the tension building in her body. "I promise. But you also need to tell me what's going on."

"I'm not just going to throw you to the proverbial wolves, you know," Frankie replied. "But I've also been finding out about things happening in our territory."

"What things?"

Frankie's face fell. "You know I love your father very much. And all of you. So much so that I couldn't bear to just leave you to be raised here in New York while I stayed in New Jersey or force you to be apart from him and Lucas. That's why we had that open border policy which allowed me to be Alpha of New Jersey even while I lived here. But it seems certain forces have been taking advantage of my absence."

"What forces?" This time, it was Julianna who asked the question.

Her mother's brows furrowed together. "A group of

Lycans have been banding together in our territory, forming their own organized group. According to my sources, they call themselves The Family."

Adrianna raised a brow. "And you didn't know about any of this?"

"I had heard of them," Frankie said. "But they didn't seem significant at the time. Frankly, New Jersey's population isn't really that big, and they managed to stay out of trouble. However, it seems their influence has grown in the last decade or so."

Something told her this wasn't going to be a fun conversation, but she had to know what she was about to get herself into. "What exactly have they been up to?"

Frankie's brows knitted together. "Illegal gambling. Larceny. Bribing officials. Kickbacks from road construction. Loan sharking. Extortion. Racketeering." Frankie looked distraught. "They've managed to stay under the radar of the human authorities thanks to bribes and connections. The Lycan High Council has turned a blind eye because they haven't directly harmed anyone or done anything to expose us to the rest of the world."

Julianna placed her hands on her hips. "So what you're saying is, *the mob* has taken over New Jersey?"

"I don't know what to say." Their mother's shoulders sank and the lines on her face deepened. "As long as they didn't hurt anyone, I thought it was fine. They've also done some good in the community, both human and Lycan. They've been known to do charity work and help people during times of disaster, like those hurricanes that devastated the shore."

"Classic organized crime whitewashing tactic," Julianna huffed. "You know, Al Capone established a soup kitchen during the Great Depression, right? And the Yakuza helped clean up that nuclear disaster in Japan."

Adrianna glared at her sister. It was obvious their mother knew she had let things get out of hand, but there was no need to pile it on. Besides, what they needed were solutions, not blame. "What are we going to do about this?"

"I'm glad you asked," Frankie said. "Because we will be meeting the head of The Family tomorrow. His name is Anatoli Corvinus."

Adrianna's jaw dropped. "What?"

"I've reached out to him, and he's agreed to a meeting. And I'm going to lay down the law." Her mother's lips curled up into a smirk. "I mean, I'm still his Alpha, and he will have to obey me. And you, Adrianna, once you've ascended to Alpha."

Julianna let out a huff. "Do you really think someone who has amassed great power would just roll over and do what you tell him?"

"He has no choice," Frankie said. "He can obey me or get out of my territory."

"I have a feeling it won't be that simple." She didn't want to say it out loud, but her sister had a point.

"That's why you need to establish yourself as rightful Alpha," Frankie said. "Consolidate and build your power. The first thing we're going to do is have you establish your own Lycan security force. I've already sent out feelers that we're looking for candidates. We'll make it official as soon as we can, no need for fancy balls or ceremonies."

"I want to help," Julianna said. "I've been part of the New York Lycan Security Force for six years. And I've been trained by the best."

Frankie smiled at her middle daughter. "I was hoping you'd say that."

"This could be a new era for our clan. We could make things better and get rid of those scumbags." For once during this entire conversation, Julianna actually sounded optimistic.

"New Jersey has always been led by the strongest women in our family," Frankie stated. "And we will work together to keep our legacy."

Adrianna looked from her mother to her sister and knew her fate was sealed. It still felt unfair, this whole deal. She hadn't asked to be Alpha. Didn't want to be Alpha. But if she were honest with herself, she knew the real reason why she was so apprehensive. She didn't know if she *could* be Alpha. Doubt crept into her mind all the time. It seemed so far away, the possibility of her even becoming Alpha so young hadn't even entered her thoughts. Her mother announcing her retirement had surprised everyone, most of all her. She didn't feel prepared. Not at all.

She swallowed the lump in her throat and ignored the butterflies in her stomach. "All right. Where do we begin?"

CHAPTER TWO

What am I doing here?

Darius asked himself this question a lot recently. As he waited outside The Enclave for her to leave to start her day. As he discreetly followed her car to her downtown office. As he sat in his own vehicle, staking out her place of work, anticipating when he'd see her next.

Each time, he told himself, would be the last. However, when he found himself with free time—and even if he didn't—he drove into the city, waiting for her to emerge from her home or workplace, following her like a lost puppy. It was like he was unable to control the need to see her, even from a distance. It was torturous almost, to watch her from afar, never being able to get too close.

And now he risked being detected by infiltrating another formal occasion, and this time, without an invitation. He had managed to sneak in while the catering staff was switching the space from the ceremony to the reception. It was easy enough with all the activity going on, and it was obvious that the Lycan guards were searching for intruders who were not of their kind. The New York Lycan Security Team was supposedly the best in the world, but they were spread too thin. In fact, these past two weeks, Darius had evaded their notice. While he should be proud of such an achievement, it only angered him knowing that those tasked to protect the Alphas were so incompetent and that *Adrianna* was being left so vulnerable.

"Excuse me. Do I know you?"

Darius turned around, staring down at the man who dared intrude into his personal space. His inner wolf growled, but he tamped down the animal's irritation. Realizing who the man was, he knew there was only one thing he could do. "No," he answered quickly. "You don't." He pivoted on his heel and headed toward the exit.

The elevator would be faster but physical exertion could help soothe his agitated wolf, so he chose the stairs, taking them two at a time as he made his way down from the rooftop level to the ground floor.

He didn't want to leave the wedding reception. His wolf didn't want to leave. But seeing as the groom himself spotted him, it would soon become obvious that Darius was a gatecrasher. He had to leave now.

He picked up his pace as he burst through the exit door. Instead of heading to his parked car two blocks away, he found a shadowy spot across the street and hid himself in the darkness. The snow continued to swirl around him, but the chill he felt was brief as his Lycan blood quickly adjusted to the temperature.

From his vantage point, he could clearly see who came in and out of the nondescript Brooklyn warehouse. He had prepared himself for the long wait; the revelry was in full swing after all. Which was why he was surprised when he spotted her and another woman leaving the building not even half an hour after he'd left.

Adrianna Anderson held her wool coat tight around her as she stood under the small awning covering the main entrance of the warehouse. The woman beside her looked around impatiently before she turned her gaze straight ahead—right where he was standing. For a second, he feared he had been discovered. However, she looked away when the black town car stopped in front of them. She opened the door and got inside, Adrianna right behind her.

He didn't wait for the car to pull away before he made his way to where he had parked his vehicle. The town car would most likely be headed back to The Enclave. He was already plotting out his route so he could catch up with them when his phone began to vibrate in his pocket.

"Yes?" he answered impatiently.

"Darius," came the gruff voice of Alexandru, head enforcer of The Family and technically, his superior. "Where are you?"

"In Brooklyn. On business." The Family had lots of *business* across New Jersey and New York, so it wasn't out of the question that he could be in Brooklyn.

"Finish up and come home. Now."

That did not sound like a request, and he knew better than to think it was. "Of course. I'm on my way." He put the phone back into his jacket pocket. He glanced across the street. The town car was long gone now. Even if he caught up, The Enclave was the opposite direction of where he needed to be. His wolf urged him to follow her, but he just couldn't. He needed to go back home.

"Home" or the closest thing to a home Darius had, was a small town in the middle of nowhere in New Jersey. Wakefield was a three-hour drive from Manhattan, in the midst of the industrial section of the Garden State. It was the perfect place to stay hidden while still being close enough to where the action happened. As he approached The Family's compound, the large metal doors swung open, allowing him to enter and head straight for the parking garage.

Alexandru was already there next to his usual spot, his face stony and serious. But he wasn't alone. Darius let out a snort of irritation when he saw who else was waiting for him when he pulled in.

"Hello, Darius," came the low, seductive voice that greeted him as he got out of the vehicle.

"Mila." He nodded toward the female Lycan in acknowledgment and nothing more. He turned to Alexandru. "Is he in his office?"

"Yes." The enforcer cocked his head toward the door. "We should go now."

Mila pouted, her red-painted lips pulling down at the corners. "When are you going to give me a ride in your car?" Her nails, which matched her lipstick, scraped down the hood as she approached him.

Darius lived a spartan life, in a single, sparsely furnished room in the compound. However, the shiny, steel gray Dodge Charger was his prized possession. It was the one thing he owned that was of any value, and his first purchase when his share of the business was large enough. It took the dealer a while to track down the exact color, but it was worth it. It had been the fulfillment of a promise, the American dream his father had sold to them before leaving his family in that poor village.

"Well?" Mila said impatiently. "Are you going to do it?"

"What?"

"Give me a ride?" Her hand reached out to touch his chest, her nails like talons as they came upon him.

He didn't miss her wicked smile or the sensuous tone of her voice. Letting out an impatient grunt, he grabbed her wrist, pulling her away. "Perhaps another time. Anatoli is waiting for me."

"Fine." She flipped her hair. "Don't wait too long to invite me for that drive." She turned around to walk away, her full hips swaying with purpose as she teetered on her spiky heels.

He wasn't sure why, but Mila's attentions had recently

turned on him, having already cycled through most of the single males in The Family. He ignored her, but short of outright telling her to leave him alone, she didn't seem to take the hint that he was not interested.

Alexandru raised a thick brow at him. "Are you ever going to give in to her?"

"Would you?"

The head enforcer gave him a grim smile. "She's not interested in me. You know she prefers her studs young and virile."

"You're not exactly old and decrepit," Darius added. In fact, Alexandru was in better shape than most men his age. He was only an inch shorter than Darius but just as wide and covered in even more ink. He was, as many would say these days, a real silver fox, with his thick head of gray hair and a full beard.

"But I'm not stupid," Alexandru said with a quirk of his brow. "And neither are you." True, they were both serious and all business. Which is why they occupied the second and third spots in The Family's hierarchy. "Still, you know she always gets what she wants."

Maybe if he was bored enough, he might fuck her just so she could move on to her next conquest and stop bothering him. His inner wolf reacted violently at the thought. *Strange.* His wolf usually couldn't care less about who he slept with.

Alexandru gave him a pointed look, but said nothing.

"Come." He stretched his neck to the side, cracking the

tight muscles. "My uncle is waiting. And you know he doesn't like to wait."

The two men headed inside, deep into the recesses of the compound. Over the years as The Family's influence and wealth grew, they were able to increase the size of their headquarters, adding more and more space for living quarters, training areas, and of course, storage for whatever illicit wares they were trading in at the moment.

After walking through the maze-like hallways, they found themselves right at the heart of the compound, just outside Anatoli Corvinus's office. Alexandru had barely raised his fist to knock when a gravelly voice shouted, "Come in!"

Darius followed behind the head enforcer and stood right in front of the solid mahogany desk in the middle of the room. Despite the disorganized maze of the compound and its nondescript appearance from the outside, the office was richly appointed and lavish to the point of being tacky—rich, dark paneling, gold trimmed everything, animal print rugs and even a velvet wingback chair next to a fake fireplace. Of course, as head of The Family, Anatoli Corvinus could decorate his den as he pleased.

"Sir," Alexandru greeted. Darius, meanwhile, chose to bow his head at Anatoli.

"Take a seat. Both of you." Anatoli leaned back in the large leather office chair behind the desk, his massive hands gripping the arms so hard the wood protested under his grip.

Settling into his seat, he searched his uncle's face, from his light brown brows to his crooked nose down, to his thick jaw. Searching for what, he didn't know. Maybe something familiar or a trace of his own father. They had the same size and bulk, however, that was about it. But then again, Anatoli and Demetri Corvinus were only half brothers.

"You're probably wondering why I've summoned you both here," Anatoli began. His dark green gaze bore right through him. "I'm here to discuss the Alpha."

For a moment, his heart stopped. Did his uncle know that he'd been following Adrianna Anderson all this time? Did he suspect anything was amiss?

"Frankie Anderson has reached out to me and invited me for an audience," Anatoli continued.

Relief swept through his body and his muscles relaxed. "She knows about us?" As far as he knew, no one knew about The Family.

"She *is* Alpha," Anatoli said. "She knows everything."

"Which means that is not an invitation." Alexandru scowled. "It is a command."

"Female Alphas. Hmph," he spat, a distasteful look on his face. "But then again, this is why my father, your grandfather," he eyed Darius, as if reminding him of the blood they shared, "chose New Jersey as the place to build his empire. With that bitch in heat focused on nothing else but being mounted by her mate and popping out his pups, she all but abandoned this territory, making it ripe for the taking."

His uncle's vile words left a terrible taste in his mouth,

but he swallowed it down. To Anatoli, all female Lycans were bitches to be bred, so he tried not to take it personally. "So, why did you need to talk to me?"

"Because I want you there, my boy." Anatoli said. "When I meet the Alpha."

"Me?" He looked at Alexandru. "He is your second."

"Which is why I need him here," Anatoli said. "Besides, you've had previous run-ins with them, and what you know and see might prove useful."

He had reported what had happened during the failed ascension ball, but left out the part about the Alpha's daughter. "Then I will be there." Coming from Anatoli, this was not a request.

"Do you think the Alpha will try to make us stop our business?" Alexandru asked.

"I know she will. But don't worry, I have a plan in place. A plan that will ensure our future is secure, no matter who is in power." Anatoli's expression darkened.

He felt a tick in his jaw. "What plan?"

"You will all know when the time is right, but for now, we must use this opportunity to gather intelligence and find out what *our Alpha* wants," he said, distaste dripping from his tone.

Anatoli was cruel and harsh, but he wasn't stupid. He knew real power came in the form of what you know, who you know, and what you knew about them. That was why The Family became so successful under his leadership. Despite his differences with his uncle, Darius respected that.

"So," Anatoli turned to the leather-bound book on his desk, "we meet tomorrow evening at eleven o'clock at Muccino's Italian Restaurant in Barnesville, New Jersey."

"I shall be there," Darius declared. "Is there anything else?"

"No." Anatoli gave him a wave, signaling that he'd been dismissed. "You may leave. Alexandru, you and I need to have a talk about Councilman Evers ..."

He gave his uncle a nod and got up, then strode out of the office. So, tomorrow he was meeting their Alpha. He wondered if Anatoli would be able to contain his hatred enough to treat Frankie Anderson like an Alpha. As the ruler of this territory, she would have every right to kick them out, and she would be backed by the Lycan High Council. In fact, she could send them all to the Lycan prison facility in Siberia if they didn't obey her.

Tomorrow would certainly be interesting. If they survived.

CHAPTER THREE

Frankie had set the meeting with Anatoli at the original Muccino's Italian Restaurant in New Jersey after-hours. As she went about her work day, Adrianna had tried not to think about it, but her busy mind would eventually go back to the topic. What would the mob boss be like? Would he agree to their terms? Would she and her mother be able to pull off the plan they had concocted?

Her position as president of Muccino International demanded all her time, and it wasn't unusual for her to work past nine o'clock most evenings, though today seemed extra long. She was glad when after she had sent off the last of her emails, Julianna arrived at her office to pick her up so they could drive from Manhattan to New Jersey.

When they got there, the restaurant was empty, the entire place scrubbed clean for the day, and their employees had left long ago. Frankie was already there waiting for them, and they went over what they were going to say. It would be a gamble, but hopefully, one that would pay off.

"He's here," Frankie declared as they heard the sound of a car pulling into the driveway. "Now we wait."

They positioned themselves in one of the circular booths in the dining room, with Frankie in the middle and Adrianna on her right and Julianna on her left, spread out so they occupied the entire seating area. From across them, they placed a lone, uncomfortable chair. They didn't take out any food or drink, not even a glass of water for their "guest."

"Should we greet them?" Julianna stood up, but Frankie placed a hand on her arm.

"No. Let them come to us."

She had to admit that her mother was smart. Having the meeting here and setting the scene was meant to put Anatoli Corvinus in his place and show him exactly who was in charge. Being a female in a male dominated industry, she knew how small things like these mattered, to gain respect and demonstrate to others they were not messing around. She'd always thought her father was the master negotiator, but clearly, Frankie Anderson was not one to be trifled with.

Minutes ticked by, and the front door remained closed. If Anatoli Corvinus was waiting for a welcoming committee, he would be sorely disappointed as they all stayed seated. Finally, the door swung open.

Two men popped their heads through the doorway, checking out the place. When they spotted the three women, they disappeared, and moments later, they came back inside, holding the door open. A tall, bulky man walked in, his face a mask of irritation. When his gaze landed on the women, however, his expression turned neutral.

"Primul." His thick accent rolled over the *r* as he used the formal title Lycans called their Alpha. "It is an honor to be invited to meet with you." He gave Frankie a deferential bow. "I hope you don't mind if I say that I was ... surprised by your request."

Frankie gestured to the chair. "Anatoli Corvinus, thank you for accepting my invitation. As I've mentioned, I have my daughters with me. This is Julianna, my middle daughter, and as you know, Adrianna is my heir and will be taking over soon."

"An honor to meet such lovely women," Anatoli said.

Though it sounded like a compliment, it only made Adrianna's skin crawl. She only hoped she could stay as expressionless as Frankie.

Her mother's gaze landed on the two goons behind Corvinus. "I didn't expect that you'd be bringing your ... friends." They hadn't thought to ask anyone else to be here or bring backup from the New York Security Team. But surely, the mob boss wouldn't try anything tonight, would he? Frankie was his Alpha. If he tried to hurt them, there would be hell to pay.

"They can wait outside then if that is your wish, Primul." With a wave of his hand, the two men marched out of the restaurant, then he took his seat. "Although, I was going to bring one of my top enfor—I mean, my nephew." His brows drew together. "But he's nowhere to be found. Perhaps he's lost track of time."

"If your nephew didn't care enough to be on time, then we proceed without him," Frankie said. "My meeting is with you. And I don't like to be kept waiting."

"Yes but—" The door flew open and all eyes went to the figure who strode inside.

Adrianna could barely contain the gasp that escaped her mouth. The man standing by the doorway was tall, which wasn't unusual for a Lycan, but built like a mountain. His white T-shirt strained against his broad shoulders and muscled chest, and tattoos curled out from underneath his sleeve, extending all the way to his wrists. When she saw the shock of silver hair on his head, she did a double-take. The man couldn't have been more than a few years older than her. His face was drawn into a serious expression, and those cobalt blue eyes stared right back at her. Familiar eyes. And for a moment, she thought she gleaned a hint of recognition in them.

"It's you." A bolt ran right through her system. Her inner wolf, normally silent unless she called upon it, instantly perked up, as if something interesting had captured its attention. It let out an inner growl that was so loud in her ears, she feared everyone else heard it.

The room suddenly felt too small and she couldn't breathe. Flashes of her dream came back to her. Strong arms wrapped around her. His skin smelling all male with a hint of vanilla. The bird tattoo on his left wrist. The feel of electricity when his fingers touched her cheek. And those eyes.

"You know this man, Adrianna?" Frankie's gaze zeroed in right at her.

"Yes. I mean ... no?" She buried her face in her hands. Oh, God, she was going crazy. She didn't know this man, but yet she *did*. Those half-formed dreams she'd been having were coming back. "I remember now." She lifted her head tentatively to face him. "You were at the ascension ceremony."

"Darius?" Corvinus seemed confused as well. "What is going on?"

The expression on his handsome face remained impassive, but a muscle in his jaw ticked. "I was at the ball. Remember, Uncle? You sent me. She must have seen me there. As a guest." He too, had an accent, but it wasn't as thick as Corvinus's.

"It's not just that," Adrianna insisted. "You took me away."

"Took you away?" Frankie's voice rose by a decibel. "Where?"

"I mean ... everything from the time of the explosion to when I was revived is a blur, but I know you were there." She searched his face, but any indication that he recognized her was gone. He held the key to what really happened. Why was he acting like he wasn't even there? "You carried me out of the ballroom and brought me to the ladies' room."

"Is this true, Darius?" Corvinus asked, his eyes narrowing at his nephew.

He cleared his throat. "As I tried to escape, there were two men in my way, and I took them down. I saw a woman, and she was in my way as well, so I picked her up and then deposited her in the women's facilities before I left. I did not realize that was the Alpha's daughter."

He treated me like I was a sack of potatoes! She felt her cheeks go hot with embarrassment and anger. Her mother gave her a strange look, but she managed to compose herself. "I guess I should thank you then. Or maybe say sorry because I was in your way."

"There is no need." His eyes stared ahead, not meeting hers. "It was inconsequential."

Corvinus gave an impatient snort. "Could we continue with our meeting now, Primul?"

Frankie hesitated, but nodded. "Go ahead and grab a chair," she said to Darius, then turned to Corvinus. "I don't like to waste time or words, so I'll get right to the point. Anatoli Corvinus, it has come to my attention that you've been operating your own little criminal empire in *my* territory."

Corvinus smiled like the Cheshire cat. "My family has had a legitimate trucking and construction business in New Jersey for decades, Primul. My father moved us here from Romania and built everything from the ground up, expanding our interests across the state. We have had no complaints nor has anyone been convicted of any kind of wrongdoing, except for minor inconsequential infractions.

What's the saying here in America? Innocent until proven guilty?"

"This is not a court nor am I bound by any laws, except Lycan ones." Frankie's voice became cold, and the power of an Alpha rippled across the room. "I'm not stupid, and I've been turning a blind eye because as you said, you haven't risked exposing us to the humans. But all illegal activity must cease. I know everything. The kickbacks, the bribes, the loan-sharking, everything must stop now. Or else I will go to the Attorney General's office and show them what evidence I do have."

Corvinus's face turned red. "You cannot mean that."

"This is an order from your Alpha." Frankie looked at Adrianna. "My daughter will ensure that you follow this order. She will be taking my place as Alpha as soon as possible."

Adrianna cleared her throat. "You will give us a list of all your activities. Legal and not." Under the table, Frankie squeezed her hand and she felt the tension leave her body. "We want to know about every pie you've got your fingers stuck into. Every politician you've bribed, every kickback you've received. If you've been hustling old ladies for their pension money, we want to know it too."

"We do not harm the old, the sick, women, and children." It was Darius who spoke up, but he still didn't meet her gaze. "That is a rule we follow."

"Gangsters with a code honor," Julianna snorted. "How *noble*."

Adrianna fought the urge to glare at her sister, but

continued. "Still, we want to know all your 'business' dealings."

"And you mean to shut everything down?" The anger from Corvinus was palpable, and the tension in the room thickened. "Don't you know what that means? What about the Lycans—your subjects who live here—who rely on us for their livelihood? We have brought many of them here from Romania, and they send their earnings back home. They have families, children who depend on them. Will you take the food from their mouths, even now as you sit here, rich and well-nourished?"

"Don't think for one second I don't know how much your pockets have been lined because of their work." It was Frankie who spoke, and again, she made the raw power of her Alpha wolf known. "You've been bringing people here from the Old Country, thanks to the loopholes in the Constanta Agreement. After all, I'm the one who has given them permission to come and work here. But the agreement was not put in place so you could build your little kingdom." Her nostrils flared. "But I'm not heartless and cruel, and your people will not starve."

"We propose a compromise," Adrianna continued. "You said it yourself, you have a legitimate trucking and construction business. In exchange for you shutting down all illegal operations, Muccino International will give Corvinus Trucking an exclusive contract to ship all our products and ingredients across the tri-state area, provided you meet our standards."

"Plus, construction projects for future restaurants in

New York and New Jersey, and additional work for Fenrir Corp. in both states as approved by my husband." Frankie added.

Corvinus seemed appeased but eyed them suspiciously. "Why would you do this?"

"I know what happens when there is a vacuum in power, Anatoli." Frankie folded her hands on top of the table. "If it wasn't you, it would have been somebody else."

"And you prefer to work with the devil you know?" Corvinus finished.

"Something like that." Frankie smirked. "So, do you agree?"

"And you are to protect us?" Corvinus looked Adrianna directly in the eye. "Money is one thing, but my influence protects us. Pardon my directness, but you, who has never even lived in this territory, mean to keep the human authorities from knowing our secret? And what about the new enemies that are rising? According to my nephew, they wield powerful magic."

"We've defeated them before and will do so again," Frankie stated. "I—that is, your future Alpha," she looked at Adrianna, "will fight when the time comes."

"Yet you didn't do anything to stop them," Corvinus countered. "You are our Alpha, and you were supposed to protect us."

Corvinus was much smarter than he seemed, and Adrianna hoped they didn't underestimate him. "I will protect this territory," she declared, her hands clenching into fists.

"I'll be moving back here and taking my rightful place as Alpha once my mother steps down."

"We'll be starting our own Lycan security team, just for New Jersey," Julianna added. "We already have some potential candidates, and I'll be leading their training."

"New Jersey's Lycans are mostly families and retirees," Corvinus pointed out.

"We'll have the support of the New York team," Julianna said.

"The New York team is spread thin," Darius stated. "You barely have enough people to cover the Alpha, her heir, and the rest of your family."

Adrianna shot him a look of surprise, which he pointedly ignored. *How the devil could he have known that?*

"And how could you possibly know how to train anyone?" Darius said to Julianna.

"Excuse me?" Julianna shot to her feet. "I've been working on the New York team for six years."

Darius merely shrugged. "That does not mean you can train fighters."

"My nephew did not mean to insult you, dear girl." He gave Julianna a placating look. "He's been my enforcer for half his life, since he was sixteen. And—" He stopped short, his lips pursing together. "Which makes him an excellent candidate."

"Candidate for what?" Frankie asked.

"To be part of your team, of course." Corvinus declared. "Darius is a perfect fit."

"Excuse me?" She couldn't stop the words from coming out of her mouth even if she tried.

"It makes sense, doesn't it?" Corvinus's eyes gleamed. "He already functions as my own protector on most days, and is one of my top enforcers. You wouldn't even have to give him any training." He leaned back in his chair. "And, with these terrible mages out to harm our future Alpha, how could I not offer you my best bodyguard, to keep her safe, while you are still building the team."

Oh, no. No way. She would never have a bodyguard ever again. Not after what happened the last time. "You can't—"

"We agree," Frankie stated, cutting off her protests.

She felt the blood drain from her face. "*Mama.*"

"Adrianna." Her mother put a hand on her arm. "You do need protection. And we could use the help."

"I can protect my own sister just fine," Julianna declared.

"And who would train your team?" Corvinus asked. "Would your sister be staying by your side as you try to whip your recruits into shape?"

"He's right," Frankie said. "We accept your offer. But, what about our earlier proposal? About you turning legit?"

"We both know that is not a proposal," Corvinus snorted then looked at Darius. "I suppose we could save a lot of money on bribes if we become legitimate businessmen, eh?" Darius remained silent as a rock. "All right, Primul, I accept your proposal."

"Good." Frankie gave him a nod. "I will give you thirty days to cease all illegal activities."

"But Primul that is not enough—"

"Thirty days." Frankie's eyes glowed with the power of her wolf. "No more."

Corvinus stretched his neck, showing his throat. "As you wish, Primul. Is there anything else?"

"No." Frankie stood up, and so did Corvinus and Darius. "You may leave."

"Thank you for your time, Primul. I shall see you soon. Come," he said to Darius. "We have a long drive home."

The two men bowed their heads, then slowly backed away towards the exit. Adrianna's gaze followed Darius as he lifted his head, and though their gazes met for a brief moment, his expression remained neutral. His stoicism was starting to irritate the hell out of her.

"I don't know if that went better or worse than we thought," Julianna said wryly when the door slammed behind the two men. "But that was the plan, right? To let him keep his business while stopping all the illegal stuff? Better to make a friend than an enemy."

It had indeed seemed like a good plan when they thought of it. They knew that trying to outright put a stop to The Family wouldn't have worked, and they would have risked making another enemy—one who had the means to fight. Also, this way, they could keep close tabs on Corvinus and The Family.

"He was right though, he didn't have a choice." Frankie

tapped a finger on her chin. "I didn't think it would be that easy."

"Why did you agree to have his nephew be my bodyguard?" Adrianna railed. "You know I don't want anyone following me around."

"He's apparently already protected you before." Frankie raised a delicate brow. "Anything you care to tell me about that?"

She knew that look her mother was giving her. It was her patented "I'm-your-mother-and-I-gave-you-life-so-you-better-tell-me-the-truth-right-now" look. But she refused to buckle. "Just because he inadvertently got me out of harm's way doesn't mean I want him protecting me now."

"What is the matter with you?" Frankie asked, frustration straining her voice. "Why are you being so stubborn about this whole bodyguard thing? You've refused any sort of security detail even after two attempts on your life. Is it because of Shane—"

"Stop!" She put up her hands. Oh, God, she didn't want to think about it. About what happened in the past. It was long ago, but the guilt and pain still seemed fresh, like a wound that had never scabbed. "Sorry." She took a deep breath. "I've been fine all this time. I don't need a bodyguard."

Julianna clenched her teeth. "You can't mean to have that ... that *oaf* come here and keep an eye on Adrianna? How will we know he won't try to harm her?"

Her inner wolf protested, as if telling her that Darius

would never hurt them. *What is up with you*? But it merely yipped at her in response.

"He won't," Frankie said. "If he did, he would have already done it."

"How could you trust him?" Julianna berated.

"I don't. But I trust you." Frankie put a hand on both her daughters' shoulders. "I trust you both. Adrianna," she began. "I've seen you duke it out with temperamental chefs and asshole CEOs and you've never given up. And you, my dear Julianna," she smiled softly, "you're tough and smart. The two of you can handle whatever life throws at you. Your last name may be Anderson, but you're both *my* daughters, descended from a long line of female Alphas. And the women in our family don't back down."

Her mother's confidence shook her to her very core, and as she looked over at Julianna, she saw in her sister's eyes what she felt: pride and determination.

"Corvinus's nephew," Julianna said. "Do you want us to use him to our advantage?"

Her mother's lips curled into a smile. "Yes. Keep him close. Try to find out more about The Family. He may inadvertently give us information his uncle might be keeping close."

"Doesn't seem like a chatty Cathy to me," Julianna snorted.

"He's probably not the type to respond to direct questioning," Frankie said, then turned to Adrianna. "But see what you can get out of him."

"Me?" she asked. What was her mother suggesting?

"You'll be spending a lot of time together. Give it some thought," Frankie said cryptically.

She pondered her mother's words. As much as she didn't want a bodyguard, it wasn't like she actually cared about what happened to Darius. *He's basically cannon fodder*. If he was so good at his job, then the mages could get to him first.

Her wolf did not seem to like that one bit.

Oh, shut up.

She slapped her hand on her forehead. Was she going to start talking to her wolf now?

"Are you all right, Adrianna?" Frankie asked.

"I'm fine." She massaged her temple. Darius exuded danger, and every single cell in her brain screamed at her to turn tail. Yet, she couldn't stop thinking about him and how close they were going to be in the next few days. The thought made her body hum with anticipation.

Stop it. She couldn't dare think of him as anything else except a dangerous ally. Stay close, but not too close. They couldn't trust Anatoli Corvinus and by extension, anyone in The Family. Would their gamble pay off? She sure hoped so, otherwise, it would be the end of the New Jersey clan.

CHAPTER FOUR

Darius followed Anatoli out of the restaurant silently. The two burly enforcers who usually accompanied his uncle were already waiting by the black SUV parked by the entrance.

As one of them reached for the door to the passenger side, Anatoli shook his head. "No," he barked, then turned to him. "You drove here?"

He nodded.

"I'll ride with you. Follow us back to the compound," he told the bodyguards, then gestured for Darius to lead him to his car.

It was a strange request, but he just shrugged as he complied and walked to where he parked his car at the end of the lot. Anatoli waited impatiently, and he dutifully opened the front passenger side for him, then shut it before walking around to the driver's side.

He moved slowly, gathering his thoughts, wondering

why his uncle wanted to ride with him. Perhaps he'd get an earful about being late. Unfortunately, he had underestimated the time it would take him to get to the restaurant, but still, he didn't think he had been delayed too long.

He'd already been angry and frustrated at having to be at the ridiculous meeting in the first place; he was an enforcer, not a negotiator.

And then he'd arrived and saw *her*.

"Darius!" Anatoli roared from inside the car. "Stop dawdling."

He hurried inside, started the engine and then put the car into gear. He could feel Anatoli stewing next to him but didn't dare say a word. Of course, he himself was trying to gather his thoughts and control the maelstrom of emotions inside him.

Tonight was the closest he'd gotten to her since the ball. Had he forgotten how smooth her skin was? Or how lovely her face looked? And those mismatched eyes. He could barely drag his gaze away from her.

His uncle never mentioned that she would be there. If he had, he wasn't sure what he would have done. But the moment he'd walked into that room, he knew one thing for sure: Anatoli could never know about how much he was drawn to Adrianna.

"That bitch!" Anatoli suddenly burst out. "How dare she tell me what to do!"

"She is Alpha," he pointed out. "You had no choice." Empty words, but what could he say?

"I'll show her ..." A growl ripped from his uncle's throat, a sure sign that his wolf was near the surface.

"Do you mean to break your word?" His jaw tensed, wondering what Anatoli was planning. "What are you up to?"

"None of your business." He sank back into the seat. "I told you, I already have plans in place. And the Alpha and her bitch daughters have opened up even more possibilities."

His hands gripped the steering wheel so hard, he might have crushed it in in his hands. "Possibilities?"

"You." He turned to him, a smile on his face. "Why do you think I offered you to them? To play nursemaid to that would-be Alpha?" He laughed. "You will be the perfect spy."

A tightness in his chest formed. "A spy?"

"Keep close to her, boy. Listen in on her conversations and then report back to me. Do you understand?" Anatoli's voice held a graveness that he'd never heard before. "I want to know every single thing that has to do with that little bitch and her mother. Don't you dare leave anything out."

"I won't."

"I mean it, Darius." He gave him a warning look, then turned his gaze forward.

"You don't trust that they will keep their word?" he added. "That they will provide us with the contracts they promised?"

"Don't be stupid," Anatolia scoffed. "All I'm saying is that we will see how this plays out." Anatoli threaded his fingers together. "It won't hurt to be prepared, in case the wind blows in the other direction."

He knew better than to probe further, lest his uncle become suspicious. Would he betray the Alpha? Punishment for disobeying an Alpha was severe. It could mean being cast out and forced to become a Lone Wolf. Or imprisonment in the ice deserts of Siberia. Or it could even mean death. The fact that Anatoli would risk such things meant he was planning something big.

He knew now he couldn't just hide his attraction to Adrianna. Anatoli always had a deep-seated hatred for him. He never said anything, but it was there, bubbling under the surface. When Darius was fourteen years old, he had found an orphaned, injured kitten that wandered into the compound. He kept it in his room, nursing it back to health. When Anatoli found the poor thing, he had Alexandru take it away. "There is no place for such things in The Family, boy," was all he said. He never did find out what happened to the kitten.

Since then, he'd learned to never show Anatoli or anyone that he cared for anything, lest they be taken from him. Because who knows what Anatoli would do if he even showed the slightest interest in the future Lupa?

The only way to keep her safe was to sever anything he felt for her.

CHAPTER FIVE

"All right, this is the last one!" Adrianna declared as she dropped the box on the floor and then plopped down on the bed of her new home. Well, it wasn't new, per se, as it had belonged to their family for three generations. But this was the first time she would actually be living in the old Victorian mansion in Barnsville, New Jersey,

It was the weekend, but also moving day for her. She packed up all her essentials from her apartment at The Enclave and put them in Julianna's car. Some stuff she would keep there in case she needed to stay in New York, but otherwise, most of her possessions were going with her to New Jersey.

Julianna walked in and set a suitcase next to the discarded box. "Of course you left me with the heavier stuff."

"You've got all those muscles from training," Adrianna teased.

Julianna smirked at her, then jumped on the bed and lay down beside her sister. "Brings back memories, huh?"

"Yeah. Remember the time you, me, and Isabelle decided to have sleepover here when I was thirteen?"

"And Nonna Gianna caught us trying to sneak outside because we were looking for ghosts?" Julianna added.

"Oh my God, she was so mad at us!" Adrianna nearly choked on her laughter. "She thought someone was trying to break in and came out into the backyard, her frying pan raised above her head."

"And ... and ..." Tears streamed down Julianna's cheeks. "She was ... had her mud mask on and was wearing her nylon stockings and her robe!"

She howled at the memory of the old woman, standing outside on the back porch, frying pan ready to knock out whoever dared try to harm her family. Julianna was clutching at her stomach as she tried to take deep breaths. When they both finally stopped, they looked at each other and Adrianna knew she wore the same sad look that was on her sister's face.

"I miss Nonna," she said. "I can't believe it's been almost ten years since she died."

"She had a long, happy life." Julianna rolled over onto her back and stared up at ceiling. "I remember that day when she passed, and we were all with her. She said the only reason she was sad was that she would never get to see us all married with kids of our own."

Nonna Gianna was their great-grandmother's human cousin and had been a part of the family ever since they could remember. She'd actually run the Muccino's Italian Restaurant kitchen when Uncle Dante moved to New York. She was also the last of their family to live in the old Victorian house where the New Jersey Alphas had been living for three generations.

Adrianna sighed. And now she too had to move in here. There really was no backing out. She still had to head into New York every day since the Muccino International Offices were still there, but this was her home now.

It was inconvenient, but surprisingly, moving into the old house was the most pleasant part of having to take up the role of Alpha. She had always loved this place; she had so many happy childhood memories here, from Christmases to birthdays and summers spent cooking in the kitchen with Nonna Gianna and Uncle Dante. It was in the backyard where she had her first shift with her parents helping and encouraging her as she learned how to control her animal.

Moving and living here was inevitable, and the meeting two nights ago with Anatoli Corvinus only cemented this decision. Despite the rush of confidence she felt, her stomach churned at the thought of being Alpha.

And knowing Darius Corvinus would be around only made it worse.

The fact that he could cause such a physical reaction in her irritated her to no end. It was bad enough that she would have a bodyguard, but did it have to be him? Now that the thought had time to ruminate in her head, she wondered if her mother had gone insane. What was she thinking? That Darius would willingly provide them info on his uncle? Or that he would turn to their side?

She snorted aloud. Highly unlikely. The man was as unmoving as a mountain.

Built like one, too. What else about him was big and hard?

She immediately put a brake to where those thoughts were leading. Oh, no. No way. She was *not* going to go there. *Get a grip, Adrianna.*

"You okay?" Julianna asked. "You zoned out for a while there."

"Er, I'm just ... hungry," she said quickly. "How about I make us some dinner? All this moving made me famished. Mama said she had the restaurant staff stock up the kitchen."

"Thank God," Julianna declared. "Because I'm not cooking after carrying all your stuff up from the car."

"You don't cook, period. Or rather, you can't cook." Her sister's helplessness in the kitchen was a joke in the family. Everyone tried to teach her. Even their cousin, Dominic, who had the patience of a saint, gave up. Julianna could burn water without trying.

"*Gahh*, you know what I mean." Julianna pushed at her playfully. "Go on and make me some lunch!"

"Is that any way to talk to your Alpha?" she teased.

"You ain't my Alpha yet." Julianna stuck her tongue out. "I'm gonna lie down here and nap for a bit."

"Fine. Come down in an hour. I should have something ready by then."

She hauled herself out of bed and headed down to the kitchen, opening the cupboards and the refrigerator door, assessing what was inside. As her mother had said, it was indeed stocked with various ingredients plus some desserts from the restaurant.

Hmmm. She tapped a finger on her chin and saw the jars of red sauce. *Ah!* Muccino's secret tomato sauce, made from scratch. Her great-grandparents had brought the recipe from Italy and only shared it with family. Of course, she knew how to make it, but it was a multi-day process. They also had commercialized versions of it in the various restaurants they had all over the world, but usually, they had to change it to suit the local taste. These were the real deal, probably made by Uncle Dante, Gio, or Dominic. She grabbed the jar and then some flour and eggs so she could make some homemade pasta.

Cooking in this kitchen brought back all those good memories of Nonna, her family, and her childhood. She put the sauce in a pot and put it over the stove so it would be ready for the pasta. As she mixed the flour, eggs, and water on the large kitchen table, she remembered how Nonna Gianna patiently taught her how to get the consistency right to make perfect pasta. She sniffled. *I miss you so much, Nonna.* A tear threatened to fall down her cheek, and she rubbed it away with a flour-stained hand.

"Who has made you cry?"

Her head shot up so fast she went light-headed. "What are you doing here?" The shock of seeing Darius standing in the doorway made the words spew out of her mouth.

He stared back at her with those eerie cobalt blue eyes. "I am here because I was tasked to protect you. The Alpha informed us that you would be moving today, and so here I am."

"I told you, I don't need any protection," she huffed.

"Your front door was unlocked," he said with a frown. "Anyone could have come in here."

"We don't lock our front doors out here," she said.

"That needs to change."

He strode forward, his bulk making the kitchen feel smaller. Adrianna felt her mouth go dry as her gaze followed the broad length of his shoulders and his muscled tattooed arms. Today, he was wearing a dark gray shirt that clung to his upper body, emphasizing the perfect V-shape of his torso.

She groaned inwardly as she felt the heat pool in her belly. *Madre de dio,* that body should be illegal in the Lower 48, plus Hawaii and Alaska.

"Miss Anderson?" He cocked his head. "Are you all right?"

Oh, God, and he just caught me gawking. "I'm fine," she snapped. She turned around, nearly slamming into an open drawer she had forgotten to close. *Shit!* What was the matter with her? Why was she acting like a schoolgirl with a crush? *Pull yourself together and have some dignity.* She was thirty-one years old, the president of an international company, and about to be Alpha in her own right. It wasn't like she was a virgin. She'd had serious relationships in the past. But thinking about the last time she'd slept with anyone made her seriously depressed. *Maybe that's it.* She was losing her mind from lack of sex.

A discrete cough jolted her back to the present. Taking a deep breath, she brushed her hair back and faced him.

"Have you eaten?" she blurted out, then flushed. *Jeez.* Now she was acting like an Italian mother. She stalked over to the fridge and opened the door, bending down to search for the parmesan cheese.

Oohhh. The cool air felt good, and hopefully it could help the fire burning in her cheeks and ... elsewhere. Grabbing the block of cheese, she stood upright and closed the door behind her.

He was still standing in the same spot, staring at her, his face stony. Did nothing affect him at all? Was he just one big block of cold, unfeeling ice?

She turned her attention to the pot of boiling sauce on the stove. Grabbing the spoon, she put it to her lips. *Perfect.* She turned back to face Darius. "Do you want to taste?" She offered him the spoon.

Slowly, he stalked toward her, eyeing her like a wary animal. She extended her arm so she could put the spoon closer to his mouth. To her shock, he grabbed her wrist, sending zings of electricity up her arm, and she got a whiff of that delicious vanilla scent of his. It sent her brain into overdrive and her wolf into howls of delight.

She tamped down her hormones but couldn't help but watch as he opened his lips and took a taste of the sauce from the spoon.

"Well?" Her voice came out breathier than she wanted.

"It is ... nice." His expression turned flat, and he let go of her hand.

She felt even more frustrated at his cool indifference, even as her body reacted to being so close to him.

Darius obviously felt nothing. *And that was good*, she told herself. If this whole thing was going to work, she would have to keep him at an arm's length. Still, she knew she was attractive. An ex-boyfriend had compared her curvy body to Botticelli's Venus, and her face was pretty enough. For God's sake, she couldn't even go to industry conferences without an escort because she kept getting propositioned by various chefs and CEOs. So, maybe her ego was getting *just a bit* bruised because Darius didn't seem to have the same reaction she was having to him.

"What's going on here?"

Julianna's voice made her take a step back away from Darius. "Julianna." She cleared her throat. "What are you doing here?"

"Me?" Her sister marched into the kitchen. "What is *he* doing here?"

"Like I explained to Miss Anderson," Darius began. "I am here to protect her."

Julianna's nostrils flared. "So you say."

"I should inspect the perimeter," he said, turning on his heel. "I'll be back as soon as I'm done." He disappeared out the back, the door shutting behind him with a loud thud.

"I still can't believe Mama agreed to this," Julianna huffed.

"I know, right?" She sighed and massaged her temple. "Lunch will be ready soon. Did you wash up?"

Julianna guffawed. "Yeah. And you should think of doing the same."

"What do you—" She glanced toward the mirror hanging above the sink. "Oh, *madre de dio*!" She looked like a disaster. Most of her hair had come out of her bun, and her cheeks and temples were streaked with flour. The front of her shirt was splattered with red sauce and worse—she didn't realize how thin both her shirt and bra were, and her nipples were poking through the fabric.

"*Gahh*!" She reached for the nearest kitchen towel and wiped her face, but really, she just wanted to hide the blush on her cheeks. Darius had seen her like this. No wonder he was eager to run away.

"Adrianna?" Julianna eyed her suspiciously. "What's the matter?"

"Nothing." She tossed the towel towards the sink. "I'll finish up the pasta and we can eat soon." Hopefully this day wouldn't turn into a bigger disaster.

Darius didn't return until after they had finished dinner. Adrianna would have called him in to eat, but she was still mad—that she had reacted like some hormonal boy-crazy teen around him, and he didn't react to her at all. *He could starve for all I care.*

However, the Italian in her couldn't help herself, so as soon as he walked back in the door, she said, "I made you a plate, it's in the fridge. Now," she shot back to Julianna. "Where were we?"

Julianna stared back at her from across the kitchen table, her mouth open.

Adrianna crossed her arms over her chest, signaling that she was not open to talking about this.

Her sister shrugged and pushed a folder at her. "What do you think of this one?"

After lunch, she and Julianna had decided to tackle the task of picking out recruits for the New Jersey Security Team. Frankie had assembled all the applicants' files and handed them to her daughters so they could come up with a shortlist of candidates.

Adrianna opened the next folder with the applicant's details. "Chase Harris. Personal trainer and boxer." There was a photo of the young man, probably in his early twenties.

"He actually applied for a position in New York. Meredith sent his file over." Meredith Jonasson was the New York Security Team's second-in-command. "She really liked this guy, but they already had enough recruits for the year."

"Let's put him in the 'yes' pile. Who's next?"

Julianna picked out another folder and slid it toward

her. "Mark Jameson. High school football and track star, just graduated last spring."

She opened the folder. "He's been working different odd-jobs since then. His family's been in Jersey for three generations."

"Sounds like an ideal candidate," Julianna said.

"He seems too young."

Adrianna turned her head, then had to crane her neck when she realized he was actually standing right behind her. Darius had a plate in his hand, but was staring down at the folder in front of her. "Is that so?" she asked. "And how old were you when you started training to be an enforcer?"

He seemed taken aback by her question, but gave her a nod. "I apologize if I have overstepped my bounds. I shall finish my meal outside." Without another word, he strode out the back door that led to the porch.

She watched him leave, not knowing what to say. Did she want him to stay? It didn't seem right, having him waiting outside like some servant.

"*Ahem.*"

Her head snapped back to her sister, and she sucked in a breath. "What?" she asked.

Julianna was staring at her, her eyes narrowed. "I don't like how he looks at you."

"Looks at me? Like what?"

"Like he's the Big Bad Wolf looking at Little Red Riding Hood."

"Excuse me?"

"He's always got this look in his eye when he thinks no one is looking," Julianna said. "I saw it when he first came into that meeting at Muccinos."

"You're being ridiculous. He can't stand me, obviously. Look how fast he left."

"I know when someone's trying to hide something. The way he's so controlled around you isn't normal." Julianna glanced at the door. "Don't be an idiot, please."

"Excuse me?" she huffed.

"I'm just saying ..." Julianna grabbed a couple more folders. "Let's get through the rest of these applications, then I'll contact everyone we want to see and set up interviews. I'll talk to them first and then you and Mama can do the second round."

She groaned. Who knew becoming Alpha was so tedious? It was worse than running Muccino International. At least at the company, she had an HR department who took care of all the hiring. "Fine, let's get this over with."

At least all this Alpha stuff would help distract her. Still, she couldn't help but ponder on Julianna's words. Did Darius really have something to hide? She could always rely on her own instincts when it came to business, but it felt like she was fumbling in the dark when it came to him. He was just so unreadable.

Aside from looking over the applications, there were still so many other details they had to take care of. By the time they finished, it was already late. She got up and stretched her arms over her head. "I have an early day tomorrow." Now that she was living here, her commute would be twice as long, plus she would have to drive herself back and forth.

"Do you suppose the Big Bad Wolf went back to his house of sticks?"

She chuckled. "I think you're mixing up your fairy tales."

"Never did believe in them." Julianna got up and opened the back door. "*Jesus Christ on a cracker*!" she exclaimed, jumping back. "How long have you been standing there?"

Darius had his back to them, his large frame nearly covering the entire doorway. "I have not left at all." He nodded to the empty plate on the floor. "Thank you for the meal."

Julianna waved a hand at him. "Well, we're headed to bed, so you can go back to where you came from."

"I cannot."

"You can't mean to stay here," Adrianna interjected. "Why don't you go back home for the night?"

"The compound where I live is a two-hour drive away," he stated. "It would seem impractical. But do not worry about me. I will sleep in my car."

"Your car?"

"I've slept in worse places," he shrugged. "Besides, what if you were attacked in the middle of the night?"

"I can take care of us," Julianna huffed. "And the house is being protected by magical spells plus a high-end security system on the perimeter. The feed goes directly to the New York Security Team."

"Still, The Family has been tasked to look after you, and if something were to happen, then we would be responsible," he said. "Good night, ladies, I will see you in the morning."

"Stubborn idiot," Julianna spat. "Are we really going to let him creep outside while we sleep in here?"

"What do you want me to do? Have his car towed away?" Maybe she should have him hauled off the property. Or report him as a prowler. "Let's just go to bed. I'm tired and I don't want to deal with this anymore."

Julianna elected to stay in Uncle Dante's old room while Adrianna had taken the master bedroom in the house which had been her mother's when she lived here. It was actually a very comfortable bed, and yet, she couldn't seem to get to sleep. For one thing, her she-wolf was whining at her, not giving her a moment's peace.

She punched her pillow in frustration. "What the hell do you want from me?"

The she-wolf let out a pathetic mewl.

She plopped her pillow over her face to muffle her scream. The truth was, it wasn't just her she-wolf's complaints that made it hard to relax. The thought of Darius cooped up in his car had her tied up in knots for some reason.

"Argh!" She rolled out of bed, her feet landing on the hardwood floor with a soft thud. *I hope I don't regret this.*

CHAPTER SIX

One of the things all enforcers in The Family trained for was the possibility of being captured and tortured for information. Being in such a dangerous line of business, it was a risk. Despite all his rigorous training, Darius never thought he would be faced with *this* particular type of torment.

He'd managed to stay away from her for a few days, but mostly, that was because Anatoli was running him ragged, sending him on various errands and jobs, and constantly reminding him that his loyalty was to The Family. Finally, yesterday he got the orders from Anatoli that he needed to go back to the Alpha's home town, as Adrianna had already left New York. He was itching to ask his uncle how he knew this but knew better. However, the thought that Anatoli had eyes on the future Alpha made him unsettled.

When he arrived at the designated address, his

instincts were to immediately assess the area for threats and weaknesses. The house was old and quite massive, but it had no walls or fences. He walked right into the front door and followed the sounds of activity coming from one of the other rooms. He didn't know what to expect, but it certainly wasn't the future Alpha of New Jersey making dinner.

The sight of Adrianna so natural and domestic mesmerized him, with her skin flushed from the heat of the kitchen, a spot of flour on her delicate nose, and her hair all mussed up like she had just gotten out of bed. The way her mouth parted and her tongue licked at her lips had his cock twitching. Her nipples poking through her shirt after she had reached inside the refrigerator had him as hard as steel. And when she offered him a taste of her food and he leaned in and got a whiff of her delicious smell, he nearly lost control like some untried teenage boy. While the interruption of the other Anderson hadn't been pleasant, it wasn't unwelcome as it gave him a chance to escape.

Surely, he must be some kind of masochist, because he was looking forward to seeing her again in the morning. He didn't have to stay behind, but he just couldn't leave her. His wolf would not let him either.

And so tomorrow would be another torturous day. He would have to watch her, smell her, be so close, yet unable to touch those sensuous curves—

The rapping on the window had him bolting straight up from where he was lying down in the back seat of the car. He blinked as his eyes adjusted to the dark, and the first thing he saw through the glass pane was a pair of mismatched eyes.

"Darius?" came Adrianna's tentative call. "Were you asleep?"

He righted himself, running his hand through his hair before opening the door. She staggered back as he unfolded his frame from the vehicle to stand in front of her. "Yes, Miss Anderson? Is there anything I can do for you?"

She sighed, then bit her lip. "It's just ... it's silly that you have to stay out here. It's the middle of winter."

"We are Lycans," he said. "Our body adjusts to the temperature."

"It can't be comfortable in there." She poked her head around him, trying to peek inside the car. "It's so cramped and you're so, er, large."

"As I said, I have slept in worse conditions." He stretched to full height, cocking his head to the side. "What are you trying to say?" Even in the low light, he could tell that her cheeks were flushed.

"I ...We have five bedrooms inside. You can take the one on the ground floor. I'm sure you'll find it adequate."

"There is no need."

"Just come in, okay?" she sputtered out, then turned around, grumbling something about "stubborn men" and "macho Lycans." She straightened her spine. "As your Alpha, I order you to come in."

He should have pointed out to her that she wasn't Alpha yet, but bit his tongue. "As you wish."

She trudged back to the house, and he followed her inside. Indeed, the house was much cozier than the inside of his car, and the warmth immediately made his body relax. He trailed after her as she walked down the hallway and entered the last door on the left.

"Here," she said as she turned on the light. The room was small but neat and looked like it was kept clean. There was a dresser, a side table, and a bed, though the mattress was bare.

"The bed's pretty comfortable. No one's stayed here in a while, not since ..." Her face went all pensive and he sensed her sadness again. She pivoted and walked toward the dresser. "Let me make the bed for you." She began to take out some sheets from the top drawer.

"No." He rushed to her side. "You are to be Alpha. Why would you do such a lowly task?" His uncle employed various servants back at the compound to serve him. He doubted Anatoli had ever made his own bed, much less changed the linens.

She let out a huff and pulled a sheet out from the drawer. "You don't know anything about being a leader, do you?"

He didn't answer.

"When I was growing up," she began as she unfolded the sheet over the mattress, "my father told me and my brother that as a leader—whether that's as an Alpha or head of a company—you should never ask those under you to do things you wouldn't do yourself." She tucked the ends under the mattress and walked around the bed to do the same to the other side. "So, we started at the bottom. When we were teens, Lucas would work in the mailroom of Fenrir Corp. I worked at Muccino's, busing tables and hostessing on weekends. Sometimes we'd switch too." She dusted her hands together when she was done, then looked up at him, her face earnest. "No task is lowly, because everything contributes to the greater success of the group."

"Like a pack," he added.

"Exactly." She blinked, then parted her lips, a soft sigh escaping her lips. When had she gotten so close to him? He didn't even realize, so mesmerized was he as he watched her complete the task of making the bed for him. When her lashes lowered and her cheeks pinked, it hit him—here, in the small room, free from the scents of cooking—he could smell her soft, delightful scent, tinged with arousal.

"I should go," she stammered, moving away from him. "Blankets and pillows are in the dresser. Goodnight."

He couldn't speak, couldn't move, and watched as she disappeared through the doorway.

Had he imagined it? How could he have missed it all this time? The way her gaze warmed at him, and her heartbeat quickened in his presence. Maybe he was blind and deaf, or he didn't want to see it.

That she could even have the slightest bit of attraction to him only added to his torment. And, as his hand ran over the sheets, smelling with traces of her scent, he wondered if he would be better off sleeping in the car tonight.

"Coffee?" Julianna Anderson offered as he entered the kitchen. When her gaze clashed with his, she smirked. "Looks like you could use a cup or four." She cocked her head to the pot brewing on the kitchen counter.

"Thank you." As he poured himself a cup, he found himself regarding the other Anderson. Though she had the same eyes and a similar face to Adrianna, that was where all resemblance between the two sisters ended. While Adrianna was petite and curvy, Julianna was a head taller and athletic. Her hair was cut in a severe style that ended at the chin, practical and no fuss, and she dressed pretty much in the same way. Today she was wearing a long-sleeved exercise top, leggings, and running shoes on her feet, which were propped up on the kitchen table.

He wasn't sure what to think about her. But it was obvious what she thought of him as evidenced by the permanent scowl on her face when he was around.

"Feet off the kitchen table," Adrianna said as she breezed into the kitchen. She knocked Julianna's legs off with a flick of her hand, which earned her a scowl from the younger woman. She chuckled and rubbed her sister's hair affectionately.

The easy and relaxed atmosphere around the sisters reminded him of another time. Of a time when he ruffled the hair of someone much younger. Of blue eyes looking up at him in wonder. Of a small face with a gap-tooth smile. And then ... the blank slate of nothingness.

"Darius?" Adrianna was looking at him. "Are you okay?"

Her gentle, concerned tone brought him back to the present. "I'm fine."

"Then please be careful, that cup is very old."

He looked down at the delicate cup in his hand, his fingers gripped around the body. "Apologies." He placed it on the counter and reached into a cupboard for a sturdier mug. "Are we heading into the city today, Miss Anderson?"

She seemed to bristle at his question. "Well, I am. I have to go to work."

"Then I will be with you."

The tips of her ears went red. "It's just New York. I've been safe there the past couple of weeks. The mages wouldn't dare try anything in my father's territory."

"Still, I am tasked with your safety. I am bound by my family's oath to the Alpha to keep you safe."

"I—"

"For God's sake, just let him follow you, Adrianna." Julianna rolled her eyes. "You've already let him in the house. You know what they say, right? Once you let a stray animal in, you'll never get rid of them."

He didn't know if he wanted to thank Julianna or wring her neck. So, he decided to ignore her. "I can drive you into the city. That way, with your hands free, you can get some work done on your phone."

She opened her mouth, then quickly shut it again. "Fine. Let's go."

He walked ahead of her, opening the front door to let her out into the porch. "We can take my car," he said. She shrugged and motioned for him to go ahead. Dashing over to his vehicle, he opened the rear passenger seat. When he glanced back at her, she was frowning.

"What are you doing?" She walked around to the front passenger seat and pulled the door open.

"It's not—"

"You wanted to drive me, right? Well, I don't want to be late," she said before she slipped inside and shut the door.

He paused, gathering his thoughts. It was bad enough that he would be trapped in that enclosed space, smelling her sweet scent, but now she would be right beside him and it would be even harder to ignore her. When she walked into the kitchen, he saw the flicker of desire in her eyes as her gaze ran over his body. Last night had been a revelation and now he couldn't unsee her attraction to him. Which only made things even more dangerous.

Not wanting to keep her waiting, he slipped into the driver's seat. She was already settled in, eyes on her phone as she typed furiously. He tore his gaze away from her, started the engine, and braced himself for a very long drive ahead.

CHAPTER SEVEN

"Giselle," Adrianna said as she breezed out of her office, coat and purse in hand.

The young woman sitting at the desk looked up at her from her computer screen. "Yes, Ms. Anderson?"

"I'm headed to lunch across the street. I don't want to be disturbed unless it's a real emergency."

"Yes, Ms. Anderson."

"Thank you." She strode out the door and took the elevator to the ground floor. Muccino International had their headquarters downtown in the SoHo district, across the street from the upscale Manhattan branch of their original Italian restaurant, which was run by her uncle Dante. Ironically, the physical office itself was actually located right above Petite Louve, a French restaurant run by his wife, Holly.

She glanced around, wondering where Darius was. He had dropped her off in front of the office—she still wondered how exactly he knew where to go—and said that he would park in the back. Her emails and to-do lists were starting to pile up, so she didn't even have time to think of where he'd be while she was working. Had he decided to go home? The thought disturbed her for some reason.

"Miss Anderson."

"*Madre de dio*!" She jumped back and placed her hand on her heart. Darius stood in front of the elevator doors, the same aloof expression on his face. "Have you been here the entire time?"

"I didn't have access to get upstairs."

"Next time, just have the receptionist buzz you in."

"Shall I get the car?" he asked.

"No." She shook her head. "I'm just going across the street for lunch. Oh, are you hungry? Did you get something to eat?" She didn't really know when he was supposed to go on breaks or get meals. The Lycan Security Team always worked in shifts.

"I am not hungry," he stated. "I shall find a quick meal later."

"Nonsense. Come on." She waved to him to follow her, and they left the building to cross the street to Muccinos. They entered the restaurant, and as soon as the maître d', Jon, saw her, he rushed to her side.

"Ms. Anderson," Jon said, his tone warm and welcoming. "Ms. Hannah is already inside. At your usual table."

"Thanks, Jon. My, er"—she glanced at Darius—"companion needs to eat too. Please get him a table."

"There is no need," Darius said.

"Of course, Ms. Anderson." When Jon tried to hand Darius a menu, the Lycan shot him a freezing look. The poor maître d' looked to Adrianna.

"Fine," she sighed. "Please have some food made for him and he can eat it later."

"Yes, Ms. Anderson."

Damn stubborn man. She crossed the busy dining room, ignoring Darius, but she could practically feel him looming behind her. She went straight to the kitchen and toward the glass-enclosed private chef's table in the back.

"Adrianna!" Hannah Taylor-Muccino, her best friend and adopted cousin, greeted as she came in.

"Hey, Hannah. No, don't get up." She waved her hand. "How's Blaise?"

Hannah glanced down at the bundle in her arms. "She's mostly sleeping through the night and eats a lot."

She smiled at the tiny infant, nestled against her mom, her large, light hazel eyes wide open. "She's growing so much. I swear it's only been two weeks, but she's filled out a lot more." The beautiful little girl giggled when she reached over to tickle her.

"All the milk goes to her cheeks," Hannah laughed, then stopped suddenly. "Er, who's your friend?"

She froze, then turned her head. Darius was right behind her, his large frame towering over her. For a moment, his normal dismissive expression flickered into ... wonder? Curiosity? "This is Darius. He's my bodyguard."

That earned her a stunned look from Hannah. "Bodyguard?"

"I'll explain everything ... in a bit."

"Would you like me to wait outside, Miss Anderson?" he asked.

Thank goodness he offered. "Yes, please." She didn't need him eavesdropping on her and Hannah's conversation.

He gave her a nod and turned to leave the room.

"So ..." Hannah began as she placed Blaise in the infant carrier propped up on the chair next to her. "You finally agreed to have a bodyguard?"

Being her best friend since childhood, Hannah knew everything of course. "It's not what you think."

"Well, I'm glad," Hannah sat down and faced her. "You're so damn stubborn about this bodyguard thing. This is your safety we're talking about. Of course, if I had someone like that, I wouldn't say no."

"Excuse me?"

Her friend chuckled. "Where did you find him, anyway? Beefcakes R Us?"

"Hannah!" she admonished. "You're married, and you just had a kid! What would Anthony say?"

"What? I can't look?" She gave her a sly look. "Do *you* plan to do more than looking?"

"Oh, please," she said. "He doesn't even want to be here." She quickly explained to Hannah about The Family and how Darius had been offered by his uncle as a bodyguard.

"Ooh, a bad boy, huh?" Hannah teased. "I could tell right away, from those tattoos and those muscles. I'm not sure about that hipster dye job, though. But c'mon, you don't find him the least bit attractive?"

"It doesn't matter because he's obviously not interested."

"I don't know, he's got this vibe—"

"Excuse me, Ms. Anderson, Ms. Muccino," a female server came in with a tray. "Your starters are ready."

Thank God. She really did not want to discuss Darius anymore. "Excellent." She turned to Hannah. "Let's eat."

As they enjoyed their meal, they didn't broach the subject of Darius again. She deliberately manipulated the conversation, asking Hannah all about Blaise. It was obvious the new mother was only too happy to chat about her child, and Adrianna couldn't blame her. Blaise was adorable and very much loved by her parents. Anthony and Hannah waited almost five years before having her as he was still working on his career as a top lawyer in New York and her wedding gown boutique was booming.

Hannah wiped her mouth with her napkin. "I need to use the ladies' room," she declared as she stood up. "Do you mind looking after her?"

Adrianna shook her head. "Not at all."

"Thanks," she said gratefully as she headed to the back door where the private facilities were. Unfortunately, as soon as Hannah disappeared, Blaise's tiny lips stuck out and her mouth turned down into a frown.

"Oh, no! Baby ..." When the tears pooled at the corner of her eyes and threatened to spill down her chubby cheeks, Adrianna quickly unstrapped her from her carrier.

"There, there. Mommy'll be back soon." She brought Blaise to her chest, making soothing motions down her back, but her little body began to rack with soft sobs. She flipped the baby around so she could face the kitchen, hoping the activity would distract her. "Look, Blaise! Did you see that? It's—"

Cobalt blue eyes staring at her made her stop, and her heart gave a nervous jolt. Darius was right outside the glass windows, facing her. How long had he been staring at her? And what was that look in his eyes? His gaze flickered down to Blaise and then he turned away, giving his back to her, settling into a defensive position like he expected the mages to come bursting through the door.

"Adrianna?" Hannah had come up beside her. "Is there anything wrong? Was she fussy?"

Blaise seemed distracted by the noise and the bustle of the kitchen and had gone quiet in her arms. "She's fine now." She handed the baby back to Hannah.

"Thanks. Oh, look, my brother finally decided to show his face," Hannah nodded toward the door.

She turned around. "Ah, looks like the lunch rush is slowing down."

Gio Muccino, who ran the kitchen when Uncle Dante wasn't around, waved to them from the other side of the glass wall as he walked toward the dining room. He slowed down as he passed by Darius, his eyes narrowing at the other man. Darius paid him no mind, but stepped aside to let him pass.

"Hey, Adrianna, Hannah," he greeted, then went

straight to Blaise. "Hey, how's my *bambina*? Did you miss Uncle Gio?" He tickled her chubby belly, sending Blaise into peals of laughter. "So, who's Mr. Serious out there?"

"Adrianna's bodyguard," Hannah said.

"Really?" Gio looked at her like she had grown another head.

She rolled her eyes. "Really," she said.

Her cousin nodded in approval. "Good for you. I know you don't like it, but you really do need someone protecting you."

"I'm going to be Alpha." If her tone sounded annoyed, it's because she *was*. "Don't you all think I'm capable of taking care of myself?"

"It's not that, Adrianna," Gio began, his mismatched eyes turning concerned. "Those mages mean business. We gotta do everything we can to keep you safe."

She knew he was right. They—her parents, Lucas, Julianna, and everyone in her family—all wanted to protect her. But the fact that her safety depended on putting another person in danger was just something her conscience couldn't handle. *Not again.* She looked at Darius, who still stood in the same position outside the room. Really, she shouldn't care. Darius was none of her concern and so she should ignore the way her stomach knotted at the thought of him being hurt.

"Gio," Hannah began. "Do you have any special dessert for us? Maybe you can take a break for a bit and join us?"

"Of course I do," he said. "I'm having someone bring it out of the oven now."

Adrianna breathed a sigh of relief, thankful for Hannah changing the subject. "Good, because I saved lots of room." Hopefully there would be no more talk of Darius or the mages from now on.

They finished lunch and though Adrianna didn't want to leave just yet, she did have responsibilities, as did Hannah. With a final goodbye to Gio and Hannah—plus a long cuddle and kiss for Blaise—she walked out of the private dining room. Darius was waiting, of course, his cobalt blue gaze immediately darting to her as soon as she appeared next to him.

"I hope I didn't keep you waiting too long," she said.

"It's my job."

She didn't know if she wanted to scream or sigh. That's all she was to him. A job. But then again, why should she expect anything else? Hell, she didn't want him around in the first place. She didn't want a bodyguard, ever. Not since—

A sudden shiver went through her. Those memories came back. Not rushing, like it did in the movies, but more like a slow, ebb of emotions and flashes of scenes. A cold sweat broke over her forehead.

"Miss Anderson?" His gaze turned curious.

She swallowed the fear and bitterness. Frankly, she was surprised it had taken this long for the memories to resurface. It had taken years to bury it all.

"You are unwell. What is wrong?"

"None of your business," she snapped. Despite her acrid tone, he didn't seem too offended. "I mean, I'm fine. I just need to get back to the office." She didn't bother to wait for him, her feet practically having a life of their own as she rushed out.

The cool, winter air felt good on her damp skin. She stopped just outside Muccino's front door. Her body felt frozen. *Get a grip.* She didn't want anyone to see her this way, especially him.

A looming presence behind her told her that Darius was there. Surprisingly, she wasn't scared or angry.

"We should head back to your office. It is getting cold out here."

His words wrapped around her like a warm blanket and despite herself, she nodded in agreement. "Yes, let's go."

It had been years since she'd had dreams of that day.

Right after the incident, the nightmares had been so vivid that she would wake up screaming. Mama would come into her room and rock her to sleep while Papa stood by, helpless as he watched his daughter relive the worst day of her life.

Sometimes, she wasn't even sure what was a dream and what was real, as the bad men would sometimes turn into real monsters with claws and sharp teeth. But certain details never changed.

She and Lucas were waiting outside the school. Shane, their trusted bodyguard and caregiver, was pulling up to the driveway to pick them up. He got out of the driver's side and waved, flashing them a sunny smile.

The sound of tires screeching made him turn around. Suddenly, he pivoted and ran towards them. "Lucas! Adrianna!"

He reached them before the bad men did and gathered them into his arms. However, there were too many of them, and they were surrounded. She screamed as she was yanked away. Shane reached into his jacket for his gun but was too late. The echo of the gunshots rang in her ear and when she looked at Shane, she saw the red stain bloom on his pristine white shirt. She looked down at his face, ashen as the blood began to leave his body. But it wasn't Shane's face she saw. It was Darius.

She let out a strangled cry, her body jerking awake. It *was* just a dream. She rolled out of bed, her heart pounding like a hammer in her chest. Usually, the knowledge that she was here, in the present, and that everything was okay—they had been rescued from that dank basement by Uncle Nick and Meredith, and that Shane survived and was now retired with his wife in upstate New York—was enough to calm her down.

But this dream was different. And even now, in the darkness of her bedroom, she couldn't scrub the image of Darius dying.

No!

She ran out of the bedroom, down the steps, and out

the back door, not caring that she was in her sleep shirt or that the ground underneath her bare feet was frozen solid. Her lungs squeezed inside her chest, making it hard to breathe, even though the air outside was crisp and fresh. Her inner wolf seemed confused too. It didn't know why she was scared and why she had those dreams, having only been born inside her years after the incident. It clawed at her, wanting to protect her.

"*Stop!*"

That voice. A deep baritone that plucked at her, making her halt. When she turned around, she saw him. He was wearing only dark sweatpants, and as her eyes adjusted to the darkness, she couldn't help but run her gaze over his muscled body. His tattoos ran from wrist to wrist, crossing over his arm and across the top of his wide chest. She looked up to his face and saw Darius's cobalt blue eyes glowed in the dark, burning with ... anger?

"What were you thinking?" he growled. "Just running away in the middle of the night without letting me know? What if there were mages lurking about?" He grabbed at her arm.

"Leave me alone!" She evaded his grasp. "I don't owe you any explanation!"

"I'm here to protect you! How can I do that if I do not know where you are?" The anger radiating off him was so strong, she could feel it. "Are you so eager to die?"

"I don't care!" she spat. "I just don't want you to—" She covered her mouth with her hand. No, she couldn't say it. Wouldn't say it. The tears burned at her throat, but she refused to speak.

His expression turned soft. "Adrianna." That sound of her name on his lips shot a bolt of electricity through her. "What made you run? Why are you shivering, despite the fact that your Lycan body should help keep you warm?" He drew closer, so near that she could get a hint of his vanilla scented skin. "What has scared you?"

The soft glow of his eyes entranced her. "Shane."

"This ... Shane has scared you?"

"No, no. He was our bodyguard and our manny." He seemed confused, so she explained. "Male nanny. He'd been taking care of me and Lucas since we were four."

His hands clenched at his side. "Did he hurt you?"

"What?" She was horrified at the thought. "No!"

"Then what's wrong?"

"He ..." She expelled a long breath. "He was shot. When we were younger, some men tried to kidnap me and Lucas, and he tried to protect us, but he got hurt."

"Did he die?"

"He almost did," she said. "But it was bad. They shot him three times. The last bullet came close to his neck and left him paralyzed." Shane had been all smiles, but the news that he would never walk again or be able to have children must have destroyed him and his wife. And it was all her fault.

"He was human?"

"Yes."

He was silent as if pondering her words. "So, this is

why you are so resistant to having a bodyguard? Because you are afraid that someone else would get hurt protecting you? Adrianna ... this is what we do. Shane, the Lycan Security Team, and myself, we all risk our lives to protect those we serve."

I don't want you to get hurt! The words in her head sounded so loud, she thought he had heard it.

He took a step closer. "What can I do to help calm your nerves? It is getting late and you should get some sleep if you are to work tomorrow."

"I just ..." A warmth washed over her, and she felt her inner wolf whining, asking to be let out. How long had it been since she'd shifted? Too long. She didn't have that luxury, living in New York. "I think to change. And run."

His eyes flashed like brilliant blue bulbs. "Then do it. Allow your she-wolf to run free. I shall watch over you and protect you."

Did she dare? It seemed like she didn't have a choice though as her wolf was practically leaping at the surface. Her eyes were probably glowing too.

She nodded at him, then turned around to dart into the thicket of trees. As soon as she was far enough away , she whipped her sleep shirt off and allowed her wolf to take over. Her muscles crawled as her limbs stretched and fur burst from her skin. She fell forward, large paws landing on the ground, and hind legs pushed the wolf's formed body to leap over a fallen log.

Instinct took over; this was the place where she had first met her wolf, all those summers ago when she came here to learn how to shift. It had been a while, but she could remember every inch of these woods.

The cool winter air felt refreshing at it whipped through her wolf's thick fur. Legs pumped hard, pushing the wolf forward, running through the woods at breakneck speed. The moon overhead was only half-full, but her eyes could see everything, and her ears could pick up the smallest sounds from afar. A howl made the wolf skid to a stop. It stood very still, its ears perked up to listen closely. From the corner of its eye, a flash of silver darted out of the trees. Cobalt eyes glowed in the darkness.

Had she been in human form, she would have gasped. Darius's wolf was magnificent. It was large, like all Lycans were in their animal form, but the silvery hair that covered its body made it otherworldly. She realized that really *was* the color of his hair.

The silver wolf didn't move, but cocked its head slightly. A rush of excitement filled the she-wolf, and it turned tail and dashed away.

She could hear the pounding of the silver wolf's large paws on the ground as it gave chase. Her wolf pushed forward, feeling the thrill of the pursuit. Darius's wolf could have easily overtaken her, but it had hung back, as if wary of her. She didn't know if that was good or bad.

She let the she-wolf run free, giving it its freedom. But she knew she couldn't stay like this forever, so she steered it back toward the house. When she saw the back porch within sight, she began to tuck her wolf away.

Her senses returned to normal, the sights and sounds

narrowing back into the human spectrum. The air chilled her skin, and she cursed when she realized she had left her shirt somewhere in the woods. Naked, she padded up the steps and saw a blanket laid on the bannister. *Darius. He must have left it there.* The gesture touched her and warmed her even more than when she draped the thick fabric around herself.

She heard the sound of footsteps behind her and saw Darius, back in human form and re-dressed in his sweatpants, climbing the porch steps with a careful gait. "Thank you for the blanket," she began. "But you didn't get yourself one."

"I am fine," he assured her. "Is there anything else you need, Miss Anderson?"

Miss Anderson? What had happened to him calling her by her first name? Maybe she had dreamt that part, too. His mask of indifference had returned as well, and the smoldering cobalt blue gaze was gone.

"No." She turned around and reached for the door. "I don't need anything from you."

CHAPTER EIGHT

"I *don't need anything from you."*

Darius wasn't sure how long he stood on the porch, staring at the door with Adrianna's words ringing in his head over and over again, the look of hurt on her face stuck in his mind.

It was better this way, he told himself as he let himself inside and headed to his room.

He had lost himself in her vulnerability. It had brought out instincts in him that he never thought possible, just like this afternoon when he saw the child in her arms. Seeing her like that, her features softening as she soothed the infant, gave him thoughts that he had no right to think about.

And tonight's events only cemented his vow to keep his distance. Seeing her so vulnerable had nearly broken him. Seeing her wolf, and then a glimpse of her naked skin only stoked the desire burning inside him. It was too much, all of it, and if Anatoli found out—

His uncle would never know.

It was easy enough to remain stony and unaffected in her presence the next day. Except for the drive to Manhattan and back, they didn't interact much, and even then it was minimal. He convinced himself that her cold indifference pleased him.

When they arrived back at the house, the Alpha was waiting for them on the porch. But she wasn't alone. There was a man next to her, and they were chatting as they sat on the patio couch, a bottle of wine and two glasses on the table in front of them.

He got out of the car first though Adrianna managed to step out before he could come over and open the door for her.

"Mama," she said as she climbed up the porch steps. "What are you doing here? Where's Julianna?"

Frankie stood up, and so did her companion. "Your sister's in New York, but she said she'll be back later tonight. I've invited a guest over for dinner at the restaurant tonight." She turned to the man next to her. "William, this is my daughter and heir, Adrianna. Adrianna, this is William Blakely, Alpha of Philadelphia."

"How do you do?" he asked.

"Alpha," Adrianna began, giving him a slight bow. "Welcome to New Jersey. We are pleased to welcome you into our territory."

"The honor's all mine," he replied, flashing her a brilliant smile with all white teeth.

Darius felt his wolf's hackles raise. Not a good sign when around an Alpha, and Blakely quickly noticed his presence. "And who is this?" The Alpha wolf in him remained on guard, but restrained.

"This is my daughter's bodyguard, Darius," Frankie explained.

"Alpha." He bowed, but his teeth ground together so hard it was almost painful.

Blakely didn't even acknowledge the greeting and instead turned his attention to Adrianna. "I'm afraid I wasn't present at your ball as I sent my Beta as my representative. She told me about what happened and that she barely escaped with her life. It's terrible, all this business with the mages. My father was Alpha during that terrible time they terrorized us, and I heard some nasty stories."

"Me too," Adrianna said.

"It's one of the reasons I invited William here," Frankie said. "We need to start building alliances, especially those whose territories border ours."

"We have a lot to discuss," Blakely said. "And I am looking forward to dinner tonight."

The way Blakely's eyes devoured Adrianna made Darius think that the other Alpha wasn't just talking about the food at Muccino's. He bit his tongue and continued to keep his wolf at bay. Any insult to a visiting Alpha would have severe consequences.

"Darius, please feel free to have some leisure time."

Frankie had a sweet smile on her face, but it was obvious she didn't mean that as a suggestion.

"If Miss Anderson is not safely at home, then she is still vulnerable," he stated.

"I have members of the New York Lycan Security Team with me," Frankie countered. "They're already at the restaurant. Adrianna and I will ride with William going there."

"Surely two Alphas could protect Adrianna?" William's grin had just a hint of a sneer. "I'll make sure she gets back safe and sound."

He looked to Adrianna, who shrugged. "Let me get changed and I'll be down in five minutes."

"Of course, we'll be right here, *mimma*." Frankie said. "I hope you have a good evening, Darius."

He knew when he was dismissed. "I do have some errands to run. But I shall be back shortly, Primul." It was rude to just turn his back to two Alphas, but he didn't care. If he didn't get out of here now, his wolf was going to rip through his skin.

He got into his car and put it into gear as soon as the engine roared to life. Backing out of the driveway, he raced out, not really caring where he was going as long as it was far away from here.

CHAPTER NINE

"Really, Mama," Adrianna hissed at Frankie as soon as William was out of earshot. They had just been served dessert when the other Alpha excused himself to make a phone call. "Couldn't you have warned me you were inviting someone to dinner?"

"That's not just *someone*, Adrianna," Frankie said. "William Blakely is a powerful Alpha, plus one of our closest neighbors. We need his support to fight the mages."

She crossed her arms over her chest. "Don't think I don't see what you're doing."

"What I'm doing?" Frankie said with feigned innocence.

"You not-so-subtly asked him if he was seeing anyone and then mentioned I was single?" Adrianna huffed. "Are you trying to pimp me out?"

"Adrianna Callista Anderson!" Frankie exclaimed. "I

would never do such a thing." She took her glass of wine and took a sip. "But you have to admit, he's pretty hot."

"*Mama*!" She groaned and buried her face in her hands.

"What? Look at him," her mother nodded at the window where they had a view of William as he paced and spoke on the phone. "He's handsome, rich, and polite. A little older for you than I'd like, but that means he's established and done playing around."

"You don't know that," she said. But her mother was right about the other parts. William Blakely was wealthy and didn't say one wrong thing throughout the whole night. His dark hair had a touch of silver at the temples, but he was only eleven years older than her.

And she'd dated enough to know when a man was interested in her, and William Blakely definitely was. Unlike certain other men who turned hot one moment and cold the next.

Don't think about him. It had been her mantra the whole day.

"Anyway, he's not the only eligible Alpha these days," Frankie said. "There's Baltimore, even Rome. Alesso's especially charming, and only a year younger than you."

"And you say you're not pimping me out."

"*Mimma*." Frankie placed a hand on her arm. "I'm just saying, think about it."

"How would it work, anyway? If I married another Alpha, I couldn't just leave to be with my husband nor could he leave his territory to come here. You and Papa were lucky you were right next to each other."

"If you're with the right person, you'll figure it out. Though, you do make a good point. Maybe I should find some younger brothers and cousins of Alphas?"

She groaned. "So you *are* looking—"

"Ladies." William had returned and took his seat. "Apologies. I had to take care of some business back home. But I've settled it, and there should be no more interruptions." He glanced at the tiramisu on the plate in front of him. "This looks delicious. Dessert was always my favorite part of any meal."

The look he sent Adrianna was probably meant to be seductive, but it merely made her skin crawl. Hopefully, the Alpha didn't feel her inner wolf cringe with disgust. "Er, I'm actually full," she said, pushing her tiramisu away.

Thankfully the rest of the dinner didn't last too long. Frankie seemed pleased that William was open to talking about the mages, and they made plans to strengthen relations between their territories.

"Your dad's not going to like that I'm out so late," Frankie said as they walked out the front door. "William, would you mind dropping off Adrianna? I hate to put you out ..."

Adrianna shot her mother a dirty look. "Mama, I'm sure you could—"

"Not a problem." He offered his arm to her. "Shall we?"

She hesitated but realized she could insult him by

refusing. "You're too kind." Wrapping her arm around his, she let him lead her to his vehicle.

Frankie waved goodbye as she got into her town car and if she wasn't her mother, Adrianna would probably have sent her a rude gesture. "Thank you," she said when William opened the door to his Mercedes.

"You're welcome." He walked over to the driver's side and slipped inside.

The drive back to the house wasn't too long and soon William pulled up to the front. Adrianna couldn't help but glance around, searching for a particular gray Dodge Charger. Her heart sank when she saw no sign of it.

"Adrianna?"

She had been so distracted that she didn't realize William was outside and had opened the door for her, his arm stretched out to assist her.

"You didn't have to do that," she said, but took his hand anyway. "It's just a couple feet to the house."

"I wouldn't be a gentleman if I didn't walk to your door." They climbed the porch steps and headed toward the front door.

"So ..." Well this was awkward. William was standing there, an expectant look on his face. "Um, so it must be a long drive back for you."

"It is, but it's worth it," he said. "Your mother has welcomed me here anytime, especially now that it's crucial we all work together to stop the mages."

"That's nice. So—" His hand clamped around her arm when she tried to turn away. "Yes?"

"Adrianna," he began. "I was wondering if I could call you another time? Maybe have dinner? That is, so we talk more about how we can strengthen our alliance?"

Madre de dio. Could this possibly get any more uncomfortable? "Um, why don't you call my office?" She reached into her purse and grabbed her card, then handed it to him.

He seemed taken aback, but took it anyway. "I'll be sure to give you a call first thing."

"Well, good night then!" She quickly grabbed the door knob and scampered inside. As soon as she heard the sound of William's car pulling away, she breathed a sigh of relief.

God, she could wring her mother's neck! It was bad enough she was stuck out here in Jersey, but for Frankie to meddle in her personal affairs ... what was she thinking? It was out of line.

"You are back."

Her heart fluttered in her chest and her knees went weak when she heard Darius's accented baritone. She wanted to scream at her stupid body for reacting the way it did.

When she turned to face him, she groaned inwardly. He was standing in the hallway, his hair damp from a shower, and wearing sweatpants and a white shirt that was so tight she could see the outline of his abs. "Of course. Where else would I be? Speaking of which, I thought you said you had some errands?"

"I finished them."

"Where's your car then?"

"I parked it in the garage since there was space. I hope that's acceptable, Miss Anderson?"

Her nails dug into her palms. "That's fine." She breezed past him, intending to head up the stairs, but his hand on her arm stopped her. *Damn him!* Why did William's same gesture do nothing for her, but when Darius did it, she wanted to just melt against him?

"What's bothering you?"

Your preference for buying shirts two sizes too small is bothering me! Since she couldn't say that out loud, she stayed silent but attempted to yank her arm away. "Let go!"

His eyes grew stormy, and he lifted her hand to his nose. "I can smell him on you."

"Excuse me?"

"Was it deliberate? Did he scent-mark you too?"

"How dare you!" Scent-marking was extremely personal. Only close family members did it. Or lovers. "What are you implying?"

He pressed his nose to her wrist, and the touch sent a thrill up her arm. "Perhaps he wasn't bold enough to take what he wanted."

Anger boiled inside her. "What do you care? You don't even want me!" She cried in surprise when the words came out of her mouth. "No, I ... didn't mean—"

She was so focused on the loud thud of her back hitting the wall that she didn't realize right away that Darius's mouth was on hers. Hard.

Oh.

Oh.

His lips were rough and urgent, slanting over hers in a daring manner that made her knees wobble like jelly. He pushed her up against the wall harder, nudging her knee open so he could press his hips to hers.

Madre de dio.

His cock was already hard and the ridge pressed up against her, making her whimper in need and her core clench. A hand dug into her hair, yanking gently at the roots to tilt her head up so he could deepen the kiss. She couldn't stop him as his tongue slid into her mouth, tasting her and doing delicious things that lit up all the pleasure synapses in her brain like fireworks. She wound her arms around his neck, pressing her body up against him.

His warm palm slid up under her shirt, caressing her skin, moving to the front to cup her breast. When his thumb brushed over the thin lace of her bra, her nipple tightened. She froze.

"Wait!" She pushed against him. Oh, God, even though he was standing right in front of her, her brain was still having a hard time processing that they had kissed. "Why did you do that?"

"Why?" His voice was as tight as a coiled spring. "Because I couldn't stand his scent all over you." He reached forward and rubbed his wrists against her neck, marking her with his delicious vanilla scent. She gasped at the boldness of his gesture. "And because I couldn't keep letting you think I didn't want you. Not anymore."

"Y-y-you want me?"

"Did I not make myself clear?" He leaned forward,

trapping her against the wall by placing his palms on either side of her. "Should I keep showing you how I—"

"Stop!" She pushed his face to the side and then ducked under his arms. "I'm just ... this is going too fast. Darius, I ..." Her body was on fire, but also, she couldn't believe what he just said. "I just met you and you've been acting like you don't even see me sometimes."

"I see you, Adrianna. Do not doubt that."

God, his words made her ache, and something deep inside her told her this wasn't just going to be about sex, at least not for her.

"Adrianna? Are you home?"

Julianna! "Y-yes!"

Julianna trotted down the stairs, stopping halfway down. "Who are you talking to?"

"Huh?" Glancing around, she realized she was alone. Darius had somehow disappeared back to his room. *Good.* "Um, I was on the phone."

"With Lucas?"

"Lucas?"

Julianna's brows knitted together. "I told him to call you if he's having trouble."

"Hold on." She held a hand up. "What do you mean having trouble? What happened? Is he okay?" The alarm bells in her head went into overdrive and her instincts were telling her that something was terribly wrong with Lucas. "Julianna?"

Her sister's brows furrowed together. "I saw him today. He's acting strange."

"What? And you didn't ask him what was wrong?"

"He wouldn't tell me. But when I asked if he would talk to you, he seemed open about it. I thought maybe with your guys' twin thing, you could pry it out of him."

"He hasn't called me at all." Worry gripped her. She and Lucas talked about almost everything. *Come to think of it, it had been a while since he even texted or called.* "I'll call him."

"Just make sure he's okay, all right? Use that twin juju you have and just ... make him normal again." The anxiety in Julianna's voice was real.

"I will."

"Good. Where were you anyway?" Julianna took one step down.

Oh, no. If Julianna got any closer to her, she would surely smell Darius's scent on her. *Arrogant prick.* He accused her of letting a stranger scent-mark her and then goes ahead and does it himself. "Stop! I mean—I need to, uh, I left something in the kitchen. I'll be right up and I'll tell you how Mama roped me into a blind date."

"Blind date?"

"Go. Let me grab my things, and I'll give you all the details."

"Fine." She wagged a finger at her. "But I want details. I'll be in my room."

As soon as Julianna disappeared upstairs, Adrianna dashed to the guest bathroom. She grabbed some towels, ran them under some hot water and rubbed the wet cloth on her wrists, neck, under her arms and then her face.

Hopefully, this would remove Darius's scent from her body. Her wolf whined in protest, but she ignored it.

God, this was a mess. Darius. And now Lucas. When they had been kidnapped, Lucas had suddenly shifted for the first time. He was only ten years old, which was unheard of as most shifters changed when they turned thirteen or fourteen. Worse than that, he had shifted in bloodlust, a state where a Lycan couldn't control his or her animal and they went straight for the kill.

He had only done this two—no, three—times in his life, and during all those instances, Adrianna was the only one who could calm him down. Even in adulthood, she and Lucas had always lived close to one another, and though it remained unspoken between them, it was probably because only she could bring him back from the darkness.

As she climbed the stairs, she took her phone out of her pocket. No messages from Lucas. No missed calls. When she dialed his number, her call went straight to voicemail. Her brother never did that, not to her at least.

Her grip on the phone was so tight, she might have crushed the sleek device with her Lycan strength. She *had* to talk to Lucas. Damn the mages to hell. She would find out what was wrong with her brother, one way or another.

CHAPTER TEN

Darius hardly ever dreamed.

But when he did, it was only of one thing. Of that fateful night when he lost everything.

Maybe they weren't dreams. They were too vivid. He wasn't sure because the memories of that night remained fractured in his brain.

He was sitting in the kitchen, doing his English homework.

"*Make sure you study hard, Darius,*" his mother said in their native tongue. "*You need to speak English to make it here.*"

His father winked at him from across the table. "*And remember what I said? Once you are successful and rich here in America, you can buy anything.*"

"*Even that car?*" The photo of the charcoal gray Dodge Charger hung on the wall of the room he shared with his younger brother, Thomsin. He had seen the advertisement in a magazine and knew this was the car he would be driving one day.

"Yes, son. Even that car. Believe me, hard work pays off."

His parents smiled at each other, like they were hiding a secret.

The next thing he remembered was opening his eyes. He was lying down on sterile, scratchy sheets, and his entire body was in pain.

He jolted awake. From across the bed where he sat up, he saw his reflection in the dresser. For a second, he felt the same shock that coursed through his veins the first time he looked in the mirror after that night, when he saw that his hair had turned all silvery white.

He swallowed the lump in his throat and rolled out of bed. His heart pumped loudly in his chest, the sound drowning out everything else. He needed something to calm him. As if on instinct, he grabbed for the shirt that hung from the back of a chair. Pressing it to his nose, he took a whiff. *Adrianna.*

Her scent invaded his senses, and his heartbeat crawled back to normal. He really should toss the shirt in the laundry. Or just throw it away. But he couldn't bring himself to get rid of it, not when it was soaked with her delicious smell. Of course now, his anxiety was replaced with arousal. His cock bobbed up, pressing against his sweatpants uncomfortably.

Last night had opened up a dam that he couldn't close. He knew kissing her would be a mistake, but he didn't know how much. He had a taste of Adrianna and wanted more.

He tossed the shirt into the laundry basket. His wolf growled in anger. "*Stop*," he said through gritted teeth. It was his damn fault, and now he would have to live with the consequences. And he would have to face her now after he had slinked away like a coward when he heard Julianna come down from her room.

He should apologize for his behavior. It was not proper. The presence of the other Alpha had pushed him over the edge, but that wasn't an excuse. She was to be Alpha, and he was nothing more than her bodyguard. Plus, there was the fact that he was supposed to spy on her for Anatoli. He was actually surprised his uncle hadn't been bothering him every minute to ask for information. But he had a suspicion he would hear from Anatoli soon.

He could delay the confrontation with Adrianna, but he'd always been the type to face problems head-on. He heard her come down the stairs, probably to start her day with her usual cup of coffee. So, he walked into the kitchen, fully intending to take responsibility for his actions. He didn't expect to see her sitting down at the table, her face scrunched up as she stared at the phone in her hand.

"What is wrong?" Anxiety, tension, and worry rolled from her in waves and tinged her sweet scent.

Her head snapped up, and those beautiful eyes grew wide. For a second, her expression softened, but her worried mask slipped back on. "It's nothing," she said before turning back to her phone.

He had expected her to be awkward or nervous around him, maybe even dismissive. Those emotions he could have dealt with, but not *this*. She looked deflated and the fact that she was unhappy made him edgy. He had to comfort her, but how?

Walking over to the coffee pot, he poured her a cup and added a touch of milk, just the way he'd seen her take it the last two days. He saw a box of pastries on the counter, then fished out a croissant and placed it on a plate.

"Eat." He put the coffee and food in front of her.

She made a face. "I'm not hungry."

"It doesn't matter, you must eat." He pulled out the chair next to her and sat down. "Now, tell me what is troubling you."

She put the phone down. "Noth—" He gave her a stern look, and she was taken aback. "It's my brother. Lucas. Julianna said he was in some kind of trouble, but he won't tell anyone what. He won't even answer my calls and we usually tell each other everything."

So, she was worried about her twin brother. And it seemed like she would not be happy until she knew what was wrong with him. "Then you must find out what's troubling him."

"How am I supposed to do that?"

"Seek him out and ask him directly. Technology," he nodded at her phone, "cannot replace a face-to-face meeting." He knew it was old-fashioned, but that was how they did business in The Family.

"I can't see him."

"Why not?"

"You know why. It would be easier for the mages to attack—"

"The mages will not know where you are each and every second of the day. Besides, they have only attacked you during events that were planned ahead, correct?" He leaned back and put his hands together on top of the table. "Meet with him today."

"But he won't even answer my calls."

He reached out and touched her hand. "Then you make him meet you, *lupoaică*." Using that word as an endearment seemed strange, but it suited her. His shewolf.

She didn't pull her hand away or even flinch. "What do you suggest?"

"Set a time and place, somewhere meaningful only to the two of you. Don't ask him. Tell him you will be there whether or not he confirms."

"And we're supposed to disobey direct orders from our parents? They're still Alphas."

He shrugged. "I won't tell if you won't. But you must let me come. To protect you."

"I—fine." She puffed out a breath. "I think I know

where we could meet. I can leave work a little earlier today." Taking her phone in her hand, she typed out a quick message. When the device let out a soft *zzzzoom* sound, she put it down. She lifted her head to meet his gaze. "So, um, thanks."

"You're welcome."

Tension hung in the air between them, and it was like both waited for something to give. Would she mention the kiss from last night? Or would she pretend like it hadn't happened? Should he mention it?

"Good morning, sunshines," Julianna greeted as she breezed into the kitchen. "Wow, you guys look so serious. Who died?"

Adrianna let out a forced chuckle. "No one." She stood up and took a bite of the croissant, then a sip of the coffee. "I'm going to send out a couple more emails, then I'll be ready to leave in fifteen minutes." Her gaze met his briefly. "Thanks ... for the breakfast."

His eyes remained fixed on her, following her figure as she disappeared through the doorway.

"So, you made her breakfast, huh?" Julianna was leaning against the counter, munching on a Danish. "Are you going to make me breakfast too?"

"I simply poured her coffee and put some bread on the plate," he explained. "If you'll excuse me, I should get the car ready."

She polished off the Danish in one bite. "You do that, Darius."

Did Julianna suspect anything? He had made sure she

didn't see him last night. *It didn't matter*. Adrianna seemed less unhappy after he offered his solution. His wolf preened that they were able to do something for her. And truth be told, he would crawl over glass to make her happy and give her what she wanted, damn all consequences to hell.

CHAPTER ELEVEN

Adrianna wasn't sure why she was nervous. But as they pulled into their destination, her palms were sweaty and she couldn't stop tapping her feet.

"He will be here," came Darius's reassuring voice.

As if it wasn't bad enough that she was anxious about Lucas, Darius being thrown into the mix made her positively bananas.

He was attentive to the point of hovering around her like a nervous first-time parent. There was breakfast this morning, but then later, when they got to her office, he didn't wait outside the building like he usually did. Instead he stood inside the waiting room, right outside her door like a guard at Buckingham Palace, making Giselle nervous. He had also brought her food from Muccino's when she said she had to work through lunch so she could leave early. At five o'clock when she stepped out of her office, he dashed to the elevator to call it for her.

Frankly, she didn't know if she preferred the cold indifferent Darius, or this ... whatever this Darius was.

"Do you want me to wait here or inside?"

She was taken aback by his question as she never considered what he would be doing while she waited for Lucas. "Will you come inside with me? At least until he comes." She told herself because she didn't want to look like a loser, all by herself. But somehow, despite his buzzing around her, she found his presence oddly soothing.

"Of course."

She didn't wait for him to come around to open the door for her and let herself out. It was only five more minutes before six o'clock, the time she told Lucas to meet her. She told him in her message she would be here, whether or not he decided to come. He didn't answer, but she knew she had to be here in case he decided to show up.

The sign outside was faded, but she could still make out the "Mike's Diner" written in an old-fashioned font. When they walked inside, she was relieved to see their usual table—the third booth on the left—was empty. She immediately made a beeline for it, lest anyone grab it first, though that seemed unlikely. The place was half-empty, despite it being dinnertime. She slid into the booth on the side facing away from the door and Darius sat opposite her.

He picked up the laminated menu on the table. "What's good here?"

"Nothing," she answered. "Everything's pretty gross. Though you can't go wrong with the milkshakes." He raised a brow at her and she laughed. "I know what you're thinking. We own a successful chain of restaurants but we're eating at a greasy spoon in the middle of nowhere. You did tell me to choose a place only he and I knew about, right? Well, trust me. No one else we know comes here."

Mike's Diner was just like any other diner off the New Jersey turnpike. It didn't have any specialties nor had it been featured on any TV show, glossy magazines, or foodie blogs. But she and Lucas discovered this place the summer after got their drivers' licenses and drove to the New Jersey house for their first time by themselves—albeit trailed discreetly by two members of the Lycan Security Team. It was the perfect stop, halfway between New York and Jersey, and since then, it had been their ritual to eat here whenever they went to Barnsville.

He glanced around. The crowd was mostly truckers and some questionable-looking patrons. "I believe that."

"Adrianna?"

For a second, she doubted what her eyes saw. But he was really here, standing right beside her. "Lucas!" She couldn't help herself and leapt up to embrace him. His arms went around her and as she pressed her nose to his lapel, she breathed in his familiar scent—salty ocean breeze. "You came."

"Of course." He smirked at her. "You didn't give me much of a choice." The smirk turned into a warm smile. "Though I'm glad I did. It's nice to see you." When his gaze flickered behind her, his body tensed. "Who's this?"

"Oh." She looked back and saw Darius had stood up. "This is Darius."

Darius bowed his head. "It is an honor to meet you."

"Darius Corvinus, right? Julianna's told me all about you."

Huh. What could her sister possibly have told him about Darius?

"She said you were keeping a close eye on Adrianna," Lucas continued. "Thank you."

"It is my duty to serve my Alpha. If you'll excuse me, I'll give you some privacy. I shall be waiting right outside the door." Darius bowed his head again, then strode out the door.

"Interesting guy." Lucas had a dark brow raised at her.

"Sit," she said, hoping to not have to discuss the subject of Darius.

Lucas sat down across from her in his usual seat. "So, are we having greasy, cold burgers or soggy, salty fries?"

She laughed. "How about the usual?"

He called the waitress over and gave them their order—a vanilla milkshake for him, chocolate for her, and a plate of onion rings to share.

"So," he began. "Why did you want me to meet you here?"

"Why have you been ignoring my calls and my messages?" she shot back.

He leaned back and crossed his arms over his chest. "I'm not ignoring you."

"Yes you have," she insisted. "What's wrong?" She

cocked her head at him, trying to look him in the eye. "Tell me. You know I'll find out one way or another."

His shoulders tensed for a second, then slumped. When he finally did look her straight on, she saw it. Or maybe, she felt it. Doubt. Uneasiness.

"Lucas?" Was he having second thoughts about taking over Fenrir Corp. from their father? Or being Alpha? *Ridiculous.* Lucas had been *born* to be Alpha. He never had any doubts. But now he seemed off-kilter. "Please. Tell me what's the matter."

"It's nothing." He suddenly found the menu very interesting, despite the fact they probably never changed the items and they'd seen it a million times.

She'd seen this only once before in her brother. Placing her hands on the table, she leaned over. "What's her name?"

His head snapped up, and he looked like an animal caught in a trap. "No one you would know."

Ah, she *was* right. "And why wouldn't I know her?" Lucas kept a very small circle of friends and acquaintances. He almost lived like a monk.

"Because she's human."

"Oh." *Wow.* This was something else. No wonder Lucas was acting strange. He barely tolerated humans, much less felt anything for them.

"And she's investigating me for a murder."

"Oh." Double wow. Well, this certainly wasn't what she expected. "What are you going to do?"

"I don't know."

Self-assured, confident, and capable Lucas Michael Anderson didn't know what to do. This woman really was doing a number on him.

"What about you? What's the deal with that Darius guy?"

"Huh?" That question came out of left field. "What about him?"

"Don't play innocent with me, Adrianna." He gave her that know-it-all smirk that irritated the heck out of her. And he knew it too, which is why he used it a lot. "No bodyguard looks at their client that way. Or the other way around."

"This isn't fair." Her cheeks were on fire. Damn Lucas. He always was too smart for his own good. "It's nothing."

"He's part of The Family, right? Those people causing trouble for Mama in Jersey?" His voice took on a serious tone.

"We've taken care of it," she said.

"It's your territory and your business." He reached out and placed a hand on hers. "I know the women in our family are capable and strong. None of you would stand for me and Papa coming in like white knights, but promise me you'll tread carefully. Especially around that one."

"I—yes, I promise!" She hated to sound like a petulant child, but she also hated being treated like one. "But you have to promise me that you won't ignore me again. That really hurt, Lucas."

"I'm sorry, Adrianna." He squeezed her hand. "I swear I won't do that to you again."

"Good."

Thankfully, their waitress arrived with their order. She didn't want to press him anymore about this woman because she was afraid she'd have to open up about Darius. Things were too complicated and messy right now, and she suspected it was the same for him. Besides, it had been forever since they'd just hung out like this—teasing each other and laughing, talking about nothing. Just two normal siblings without a care in the world, like that first time they sat here so many years ago.

"Let me get this," she said when the waitress put the check on their table. "I invited you, after all."

He chuckled and held his hands up. "Whatever you want."

They walked over to the cashier and she handed over some cash. "Did you drive by yourself here?" she asked.

"No, but I had Zac with me, so we didn't have to get anyone on the Lycan Security Team to come and follow me." Their father would certainly not be happy if he found out they were disobeying his orders to not be in the same place together. "He's waiting outside."

"He is? Why didn't he come in with you?" Zac was their oldest friend. They were all practically raised together.

"Don't worry, Astrid's with him. He couldn't lie to her and then she insisted in coming. Besides, she took one look at the reviews of this place and gave a hard no. Do you want to say hello?"

"It's okay." She gave him a dismissive wave. "You guys

should go before anyone suspects anything." Besides, she didn't want to get the third degree from Zac and Astrid about Darius.

He enveloped her in a hug. "This was nice, Adrianna. I really needed this. Thanks for telling me to come here. I knew your bossiness would come in handy someday."

"Ha!" She tightened her arms around him. "*Now* you admit I'm the boss because I'm older."

"By one minute," he said. "I'll talk to Mama and Papa, and we can figure something out. It's ridiculous that we can't even be in the same room together."

"I know." Reluctantly, she let go of him. "Have a safe drive back. And call me if you need to talk. About anything."

He shoved his hands into his pockets. "I will."

She watched him leave, then waited a few minutes before leaving herself. As she expected, Darius magically appeared by her side. "Did you have a good dinner?"

"The food was tolerable, but the company was stellar." She breathed a sigh. Even her wolf was content for now.

"Someone is following your brother."

"What?" The look on his face was dead serious. "Who?"

"I'm not sure. But," his eyebrows knitted together, "it was your standard unmarked dark sedan. Like what undercover police use in stakeouts."

"And how would you know how police—" He gave her a pointed look. "Right." Knowing The Family's reputation, he'd probably been on the receiving end of police surveillance many times before.

"Should we follow them? If they are headed back to Manhattan, we can catch them."

Hmm. She was mighty curious what this mystery woman looked like, but she and her brother had a silent truce for now that they wouldn't get into each other's business. Still, she should make sure Lucas knew he was being followed. "I'll send him a message to make sure he knows." She got her phone out of her purse and typed off a message, telling him about his tail and asked if they needed help. A reply came quickly saying he was taking care of it and that she didn't have anything to worry about. Her instinct—or maybe it was that twin bond they shared—

told her he was in no immediate danger. "Let's go home."

"Of course."

"And Darius?" He tilted his head. "Thank you. For suggesting this."

"You're very welcome."

He led her to the car, his hand on her lower back. The touch sent a warmth through her—non-sexual but so intimate. He was just so kind and considerate today, and if it wasn't for him, she wouldn't have seen Lucas.

She was having dangerous thoughts, one that could have deeper consequences if she wasn't careful. As he drove them out of the parking lot, she sneaked a glance at him. His handsome face was drawn into its usual serious expression. She couldn't help but drop her gaze down to his lips—those lips that had kissed her so thoroughly last night and made her knees all wobbly. Lucas was right about treading carefully around Darius. He was right, of course. Things could get seriously complicated. But, right now, she didn't really care.

CHAPTER TWELVE

Darius didn't know what this feeling inside him was. It felt warm and tranquil. His wolf too, wasn't fighting him for once. It lay inside him, curled up and contented.

He glanced over at Adrianna for what seemed like the hundredth time since they started the drive back. Her face was serene, and once in a while, he could see the slight tug at the corner of her lips, as if she was remembering a private joke in her head. He would do anything to see her like this all the time. There wasn't even any of the contentious energy or nervous tension between them.

Had he known this peace wouldn't last longer than the ride home, he would have savored it.

"Hmm, I thought the recruits would have all gone home by now," Adrianna remarked. "Julianna said she wasn't going to make anyone stay later than five."

"What do you mean?" When he pulled into the driveway, he saw a black van parked in front of the porch. His wolf suddenly jolted into a defensive stance.

He swerved the car and pressed the remote to open the garage door before parking inside.

"Darius? What's wrong?"

This was not good. "Stay here," he said. "At least until I come back for you."

"What? No way!" She unbuckled her seat belt. "Whose car is that? Why are you reacting this way?"

"It's ..." How could he explain it to her? "I'm not sure, but we may be in danger."

"Danger? But Julianna's in there! You can't just expect me to stay in the car and sit on my hands."

"Fine, you can come, but stay behind me and I'll go inside first." He had known telling her to stay behind was useless, but he had to try.

From the garage he led her through the backyard, intending to enter through the rear door that led to the kitchen. Everything seemed normal—the lights were on inside the kitchen and he could hear two people talking inside, as well as the clinking of cups and silverware. They crept up the porch steps, and he reached for the doorknob, slowly turning it.

"What are you doing creeping around out there?" Julianna called brashly. "And where the heck have you guys been?"

"Julianna? Are you okay?" Adrianna had rushed inside, evading his grasp when he tried to pull her back. "Are you hurt and—oh! Who's this?"

"I told you to stay behind," he bit out.

"Hello, Darius."

When he saw the vehicle in the driveway, he knew something was wrong. It was one of the black, nondescript delivery vans they used for a variety of purposes, and *not* just for transporting goods.

It was obvious Anatoli had sent someone over and he had run various scenarios in his head about how things could possibly go wrong. But now, seeing who was in the kitchen, he knew it was probably much worse.

"Mila," he said. "What are you doing here?"

The woman was sitting across from Julianna, drinking tea like she was the Queen of England, a devious smile on her face. "Whatever do you mean?"

"You know each other?" Julianna asked.

"She is part of The Family."

Adrianna's gaze narrowed at the other female. "You are?"

"We don't carry membership cards or anything," she shrugged. "And I do live in this territory."

"Then you greet your Alpha with the proper respect," he demanded. "Stand up and conduct yourself properly."

"Alpha?" Mila innocently. "I don't see Frankie Anderson around."

Adrianna looked at him, at Mila, and then at Julianna. "Who is this?"

"This is Mila Georgescu, one of our newest recruits.

"I don't recall seeing her application." Adrianna glared at Mila. "How did you get here?"

"She was a last-minute addition," Julianna said. "She showed up and asked to be part of the training group."

"Surely every Lycan in New Jersey should have a chance at this opportunity to serve the Alpha," Mila said slyly.

"And she's kind of amazing," Julianna admitted sheepishly. "She kicked everyone else's ass."

Mila laughed and tossed her hair. "It was nothing, and you're far better than me, Julianna."

"But you didn't tell me the part about you being in The Family."

Mila's demeanor changed. "I know the reputation our organization has with you." She gave a small sniff. "I ... I don't want to be part of that anymore. Besides, being a woman, they treated me so badly. The men especially ..." Her voice trembled. "Please, I need to get out of that situation. I just want a fair chance. A new start."

Julianna's face softened. "Of course you'll get it."

"Julianna—"

The younger Anderson glared at her sister. "I've already decided she's in."

"But I haven't approved it," Adrianna countered.

"And you're not Alpha yet. Mama is. And I'm going to talk to her directly," Julianna threatened.

"Why—" Adrianna shut her mouth unceremoniously. "Can we talk in private, please, Julianna?"

She stood up. "Fine. Let's go in the study."

When the two sisters left, Darius grabbed Mila by the

arm and dragged her out the door, not caring at her protests.

"Darius, if you want to be rough, just say so," Mila cooed. "I like it rough."

"You may have fooled Julianna Anderson, with that 'give me a fair chance' act, but you can't fool me or Adrianna," he said, hauling her across the porch. "I know why you're here."

Mila rubbed at her arm. "Oh, are you on a first-name basis with the future Alpha now?" She laughed. "So, why do you think I am here?"

"Anatoli sent you, didn't he?" His teeth gnashed together. "Why?"

"Why do you think?" she spat. "Anatoli is not pleased with your silence."

"I've only been here three nights," he said. "What does he expect me to find out in that short time?"

"Oh? And how have you been spending those *nights*?" She sidled up to him. "Between the legs of that would-be Alpha? Tell me, Darius, what could she possibly offer you that I can't?"

"Mila, stop this. Go home and never come back here."

"Has she bewitched you?" She pressed up against him and reached up to stroke the hair at his temples. "Should I tell Anatoli how—"

"What's going on here?"

He pushed Mila away as soon as he heard Adrianna's voice. "Nothing."

"Just reconnecting with an old ... friend." Mila tossed

her hair back. "It's been sooooo long since I've been with my Darius—"

"Mila, go home!" he roared. His wolf's rage bubbled at the surface. "Now."

Judging by how all the blood had drained from Adrianna's face it was too late. And Mila knew it. She patted him on the chest. "I'll see you later, Darius." She sauntered back into the house, slamming the door behind her.

"It's not what you think," he said. But how was he to explain all this to Adrianna, without incriminating himself as a spy in the service of The Family?

"I don't care about your *friends*." Her voice was cutting and cold. "You're free to do what you want. And who you want."

"Adrianna." He placed himself between her and the door when she tried to go back inside. "She's nothing to me. No matter what she may have implied."

"You have your business," she said, sidestepping him. "And I have mine."

"What does that mean?"

But the only answer he got was the door slamming in his face.

Damn women.

The brief glimpse he had of a happy, contented Adrianna was gone. Instead, it was replaced by a cool, indifferent woman who didn't even look him in the eye. He drove her to work, as usual, but she didn't speak to him at all. She didn't even come into the kitchen that morning, and he felt like an idiot waiting there with a steaming cup of coffee and the box of fresh pastries he bought this morning from the bakery in town.

He waited for her outside her office the entire day, but she didn't come out. Before he could think to get her some food, a delivery man arrived with a brown paper bag. Giselle took it into her office, and when he attempted to enter, he had a door slammed in his face again.

"Miss Anderson?" he called when she blew past him as she left her office. "I'll get the car if you want to wait—"

"No need," she said curtly. "I'm not going home with you."

"You're not?"

"I have plans."

Plans?

"Dinner plans," she said. "In fact—"

"Oh, good," William Blakely said as he walked into the reception area. "I was hoping I wasn't too early."

"Not at all," Adrianna said. "You're just in time."

"Good," he said, flashing her a warm smile. "I was glad you agreed to have dinner with me tonight."

"Well, it was a good thing that you were in town for business," she said, returning his smile. "I'm sure you'll enjoy the food at *Petite Louve*."

"I'm sure I'll love it."

Darius curled his hands into fists at his side. "Miss

Anderson," he said, carefully watching his tone. "Will we be staying later than usual?"

"I'll be staying to have dinner with William," she said coolly. "You can go home."

"I cannot—"

"I'll take her home. Don't worry, she'll be safe with me." The Alpha put his hand on her lower back and guided her out.

Jealousy fueled his rage and coursed through his veins. So, Adrianna agreed to a date with the Philadelphia Alpha. Was it a reaction to Mila last night or was she genuinely interested in Blakely?

It would certainly serve her right if he did go home. Maybe he should go back to the compound. He stalked out of the office and headed toward the garage via the stairs, hoping the exercise would help release some pent-up tension and keep his wolf at bay. It was seething at him, angry that he would dare let another man near Adrianna.

He should have driven away from Manhattan as fast as he could. But instead, he found himself parking just across the street and sitting inside the car, staring at the restaurant's facade. His imagination was running wild, thinking of Adrianna and Blakely, cozying up to each other in such a romantic setting. How would the night end for them? Would he take her home as he promised? But *whose* home? Hers or his?

He wasn't going to wait to find out. Pushing the door open, he strode out and walked across the street, ignoring the blaring horn of the car that nearly collided into him.

The maître d' was all smiles when he walked in. "Do you have a reserv—hey!"

He pushed the young man aside and made a beeline for the corner table where Adrianna sat with her back to the dining room. As soon as he approached, Blakely sent him a furious look.

"What are you doing here?" he asked with barely masked distaste.

Adrianna turned her head. "Darius?"

"I'm sorry to interrupt, Miss Anderson, but there's an emergency." The lie slipped out of his mouth with practiced ease. "It's your sister. Miss Julianna."

"What?" She shot to her feet. "Did something happen with the new recruits?"

"I can't say for sure," he said. "But it's important we leave right away before the traffic conditions worsen."

She was already on her feet and had her purse in hand. "I'm sorry, William. But I have to attend to this."

Blakely looked skeptical, but didn't protest. "Of course, Adrianna. As Alpha, I totally understand."

"Rain check?"

"Of course. Anytime. Good luck with your crisis, and let me know if I can assist you."

"Thank you for understanding." She looked at Darius. "Well? Let's go."

He led her outside to the car and opened the door for her. She didn't even protest and slid right inside.

"What's the emergency?" she asked, her voice frantic. "Is it the mages?"

"I will explain when I get out of the city and onto the highway. It will be easier when I'm not trying to navigate New York traffic. "

She slunk back into the seat. "I'll call my mother."

Fuck. He locked the car doors and stepped on the gas.

"Dammit!" She tossed her phone back in her purse. "Straight to voicemail."

That had bought him a few minutes for now, but who knew how long before she discovered his deception. It was a good thing the office wasn't too far from the Holland Tunnel, but still, he pushed his car to the legal speed limit and soon they were out of Manhattan.

"So, tell me what happened!" she exclaimed as soon as they were on the highway. "I need to know what to expect."

He kept his eyes on the road and gripped the wheel tighter.

"Darius? What are you—" She stopped, then sucked in a breath. "You Goddamn liar!" she screeched. "There's no emergency, is there?"

It was a good thing he was already speeding down the highway when she realized the truth. And he was also glad he had a special device built in for his car—one that kept all the doors locked from the inside with the flick of a button right by his thumb on the wheel. While surely, she wouldn't try to jump out of the car while he was going seventy-five miles an hour, he wasn't going to take any chances.

"I'm going to call my mother! And my father! You're going to pay for this!" She reached for her purse.

"And what will you tell your parents?"

"That you're kidnapping me!"

"Kidnapping you?" he snorted. "I'm kidnapping you back to your own home?"

"Argh!" Adrianna continued to hurl insults at him, using every imaginable curse word she likely knew in two different languages. He remained calm throughout the drive which probably irked her more.

She must have gotten tired because halfway through the drive, she slumped back in her seat and crossed her arms over her chest, silently fuming. Darius knew he had to have some sort of plan when they arrived because she was not going to be happy.

When they approached the house and he slowed down, that's when she discovered the special locks.

"Goddamn you! Open this door!"

He slid into the garage and waited for the door to close before he let himself out and walked around to her side. He was also glad for the bullet proof glass he had installed as it muffled out the unholy screeching Adrianna was doing from inside the car.

As soon as he opened the door, she pounced at him, swiping her hands at his face. He caught her delicate wrists easily. "Stop. *Stop*, Adrianna." She struggled against him, and so he pinned her hands against the car. "Put your claws away, *lupoaică,* you've made your point."

Her eyes blazed with a fury he'd never seen before. "Made my point? What the hell are you talking about?"

"If you wanted to make me jealous, then I'm happy to say that you've succeeded."

"Jealous?"

"Yes. You don't have to go out another date with Blakely to catch my attention." *Or anyone else, for that matter.*

"Ha!" Her eyes narrowed into slits. "And then what? You get to have your Mila and I'm supposed to stay at home like a spinster aunt? What about *my* needs?"

"If you have needs, *lupoaică,* then I will be the one to satisfy them."

He pushed her against the car, trapping her body with his before his mouth captured hers. She struggled, but as he continued feasting on her sweet mouth, she melted against him.

His tongue pushed into her mouth, seeking more than just the taste he had before. Her sweet scent was being drowned out by her arousal, fueling his own desire. He wanted her to know how much she turned him on, so he rubbed his erection against her core, making her whimper with need.

He needed her bad. Needed to taste her bad. She cried out in protest when his mouth left hers but let out a gasp when he grabbed the front of her suit jacket and blouse, then pulled it open, sending buttons scattering everywhere. Her full, lush breasts were covered in a dainty lace bra and he let out a growl as he cupped them. She let out a moan when he squeezed gently, his thumbs teasing her nipples though the fabric. She looked magnificent, but he wanted more, so he got on his knees. He pushed her skirt over her hips, revealing matching panties.

"Darius ... you can't ... oh!"

The lace ripped easily in his hands and he was practically drowning in the scent of her arousal. He pressed his nose against her folds, wanting more of her smell. She was dripping wet and his tongue easily slipped between her slick nether lips.

"Darius!" Hands dug into his hair, yanking at the roots. She clenched around his tongue as he continued to slide in and out of her.

"*Nggghhh!*"

He swore he heard her head bang against the side of the roof. Sliding his hand down her leg, he lifted one foot and hooked it over his shoulder, spreading her thighs so he could press his mouth to her harder.

"Darius!"

Her hips bucked forward, and he steadied her by placing a hand on her pelvis. When she started trembling, he slid his hand down to pluck at her clit.

She let out a muffled cry, and his mouth flooded with her juices. He continued his assault on her core, licking and stroking her until her body stopped shuddering. Gently, he put her foot down and began to lick a path up her belly and her breasts to end at her lips. He kissed her hard, wanting her to taste herself on his mouth while the tang of her arousal was still fresh.

"Darius," she panted. "Why ... we can't ..."

He stopped her again with his mouth, but she turned her head away. "You shouldn't have done that!"

"You enjoyed it," he pointed out. "And so did I."

"This is insane." She pushed at his chest and then side-stepped away from him. "Please, Darius, I can't do this."

A tightness formed in his chest. "It's your prerogative to say no anytime. However, perhaps you could do me the courtesy of telling me why you would reject my touch now after you allowed me to pleasure you?"

"It's not ... I just ..." She clutched at her ruined clothes, trying to keep them together with her hands. "I don't do stuff like this. Despite what I said about having needs, I've only had serious relationships. Two ever. I don't do hookups."

He grabbed her hand and pressed it to his raging erection. "You want me. And I want you. This doesn't have to be complicated. We could just be two people who could give each other mindless pleasure."

"It's already complicated!" She yanked her hand away from him. "I can't sleep with you and act like nothing happened afterwards, then watch you chase after someone else! I think I'm—" She covered her hand with her mouth. "Darius, it would *destroy* me."

Her words should have elated him. She all but admitted to having deeper feelings for him. But her confession struck true terror into him. *Anatoli*. Oh, what his manipulative and power-hungry uncle would do if he found out Adrianna cared for him.

"I understand. Forgive me, Miss Anderson." He bent his head respectfully. "I didn't mean to overstep my bounds."

He slipped out of the door, not wanting to look at her face. He could already feel her she-wolf shrinking back at his rejection. His own animal cried out in desperate need.

No, it wasn't a rejection. He couldn't bring himself to say the words. Truth be told, there was something else that scared him, and not just the threat of what Anatoli would do to her. She wanted romance. Soft words and gentle touches. She deserved all that and more. But he couldn't give her that. He simply wasn't capable as he had lost the ability to care for anything or anyone on that fateful night long ago.

He dashed into the woods, ripping his clothes off as fast as he could, barely making it into the line of trees as his wolf burst from his skin. *Run.* The exercise would help burn off the excess energy and appease his wolf's rage. It had to, because he didn't know how he would survive the rest of his time here.

CHAPTER THIRTEEN

His wolf ran for what seemed like hours. He gave the wolf his mind and body, because it would surely drive him mad to have to think about Adrianna. On and on, not stopping, until eventually, their body gave in, and its legs collapsed sending him tumbling into frozen ground.

It probably snowed sometime in the middle of the night because when he woke up, the ground was dusted with powdery ice. He shook the flakes that had gathered in his hair and realized he was back in his human body. With a groan, he got to his feet, rubbing his eyes.

He trudged through the woods, and it took him a good while before he found himself back at the house. He thought to go back inside but realized that he wasn't prepared to face Adrianna again.

Maybe, this was his chance to go back to Anatoli and tell him that he couldn't get any information from Adrianna. Perhaps he could even convince his uncle that he had tried to seduce her and she was the one that rejected him. Better for Anatoli to think that Adrianna was a cold uptight bitch who hated men.

He located his discarded pants and put them on, then headed for the garage and got into his car. He drove two hours to the compound, but as he pulled into the long driveway that led to the gate, a black van approached from the opposite direction, then stopped right in front of his car, blocking his way.

"What the fuck are you doing!" he shouted at the driver as he got out of the car. "What's the meaning —Mila?"

"Darius! I'm so glad to see you," Mila said as she rushed out of the driver's side of the van.

"I do not have time for your bullshit today. Get out of my way. I need to see Anatoli."

"No!" She grabbed his arm, yanking him back when he tried to get past her. "What are you doing here? Where is Adrianna? Are you going back to her afterwards?"

"It's none of your business."

"No! You can't go back to her!"

While he knew she wouldn't like him going back to Adrianna, there was something about her tone that said it wasn't because of jealousy. There was a tinge of real fear in her voice. "And what if I do go back to her?"

"Do not! Not if you value your life." There it was again, her scent covered with a sheen of distress.

"What do you know?" he roared, grabbing her arms. "Tell me."

"I was driving back to warn you!" She looked at him with pleading eyes.

"Warn me about what?"

"I only overheard ... Anatoli said he would be taking care of the Alpha's heir today. And I was scared that you would be in the way." She slid her hands up his chest, cupping his jaw. "Please Darius. I don't want you to get hurt too."

He couldn't believe what he was hearing. Anatoli really did mean to harm Adrianna. But why? It didn't matter. Rage burned through him, and his wolf urged him to leave and go to her. "Do not tell anyone I was here," he warned Mila.

"Or what?"

"Or I will tell Anatoli you were eavesdropping and you warned me about any impending attack on Adrianna."

He didn't wait for her to protest. Instead, he hopped back into his car and backed it up, driving toward the highway like the devil himself was at his back.

What was Anatoli going to do? Real fear gripped him. Where was Adrianna now? He reached for his phone and dialed her number. No answer. Of course, she could be mad about last night. He tried the office, but it rang and rang, and no one answered. Strange. Giselle was usually efficient. Now he was really worried.

It would take him at least three hours to get to Manhattan, and probably more if he hit the traffic going into the city. Adrianna might not even be there. He didn't know who else to call.

Wait.

There was one another number that he had programmed into his phone. He said a quick prayer before hitting the dial button.

"Hello?" came Julianna's voice.

"It's me, Darius," he said. "Where is she?"

"So, did you change your mind?" Loathing dripped from every word that Julianna uttered.

"Change my mind?"

"Adrianna said you decided to leave and go back to your uncle."

"We had a misunderstanding," he said. "Where is she?"

She let out a *harrumph.* "There was an emergency," she said.

"What emergency?"

"Not that you would care, but there was an explosion in Muccino's in Washington D.C. She left at around three o'clock this morning. It's an all hands on deck type of situation."

"Is she all right?"

"Probably overworked, but yeah. But she's staying there tonight."

Maybe this emergency was a blessing in disguise and it would be better if she were far away from New Jersey, where Anatoli wouldn't be able to get to her. "I should go see her and make sure she's ... protected."

"You stay away from her," Julianna bit out. "I don't care what misunderstanding you had, but she was not herself when she came in last night. I don't know what happened, but I know you had something to do with it."

"Your sister can tell me herself if she wants me to stay away," he said. "Right now, her safety is my priority." He turned the phone off and tossed it onto the passenger's seat. He pressed his foot to the pedal and kept his eyes on the road. *Please*, he said to any god who could hear him. *Let her be safe.*

CHAPTER FOURTEEN

Adrianna had never been so exhausted in her entire life. The call came in shortly after midnight. It was a good thing she'd been tossing and turning for hours when her phone rang, but she didn't expect to be brought out of bed in such a panic.

Sometime after midnight, a gas line exploded in the kitchen of Muccino's in D.C., just as the crew was cleaning up for the evening. Four workers had died and half a dozen more hurt. Her mother and uncle Dante were both in Rome, so she was the only one who could go there to deal with the crisis.

The plane was fueled and ready in record time, and she made it to D.C. in the wee hours of the morning. It was a good thing she and her family had good relations with Senator Gerald Burns, the Alpha of Virginia and D.C, so she was able to come and go into the territory without having to ask for permission to enter. The senator even had a car ready to pick her up and bring her into the city.

There was no time to wallow in pain or soothe her aching heart because she was the face of the company now; she had to be strong for her employees and their families. There were press statements to approve, news interviews to schedule, calls to take and field, and more important, employees to visit in the hospital and grieving families to console. Compared to their suffering, the pain in her heart at Darius's rejection couldn't come close. Besides, it was her own damn fault for letting her feelings get too deep when it was obvious he was only after one thing this whole time.

"Ms. Anderson?"

She looked up at Joan Miller, the manager of the D.C. Muccino's branch. The middle-aged woman looked worse for wear, but she imagined she looked pretty similar herself. "You should go home, Joan."

"I will if you will," she said.

She gave her a weak smile. "I'm almost done, I swear."

"Do you want me to walk you to your hotel?"

"I'm fine. Now go. Your kids are waiting for you," she urged.

"All right, but be careful," Joan warned. "It's pretty slippery out there."

"I will."

The fire department had closed down the entire building where the restaurant was located so she didn't have an office, but the PR company they hired, Emerson

Communications, offered one of their conference rooms as a temporary office and headquarters while they managed this crisis.

It wasn't very late, probably only after eight o'clock in the evening, but it was already dark, and snow had begun to fall again. Also, she realized that she hadn't slept in over twenty-four hours, and she was dead tired. Emerson Communications had booked her a hotel suite nearby, so it would be a quick walk and then she could collapse into bed and put this day behind her.

She shut down her laptop, packed up her things and grabbed her coat, then made her way outside. The Meridien D.C. Hotel was on the same block, and she was glad it was only a short walk. She entered the lobby and headed straight for the elevators.

As she waited for the first available car, she took out her phone, checking her email and news alerts for any mention of the explosion. When she heard the sound indicating the arrival of the elevator car, she walked straight into it without looking up.

"Excuse you," she muttered as she felt someone jostling her. When she turned around to face the front, there were four men taking up the bulk of the entire elevator. "Penthouse, please," she said. None of the men pressed the button, so she cleared her throat. "Penthouse," she said in a louder voice. One of the men turned to press the "B" button. "Hey! What are you—mmm!"

The scream she tried to let out was muffled by a large hand that covered her mouth. Her heartbeat spiked, and she tried to get free, but two strong arms wrapped around her and she felt a small prick at the base of her neck.

Madre de dio. She was being kidnapped.

Whatever they injected into her was making her woozy and she struggled to keep her eyes open. Her feet left the ground, and the man who held her lifted her up over his shoulder.

Stay awake! She took in small gulps of air. Her Lycan system would quickly get rid of the drug in her body, then she could shift into her wolf form and run away. But for now, she had to keep making them think she was out. Technically, it was forbidden to shift in front of humans except in cases of extreme emergency, but she was pretty sure this counted.

"Grab the car and pop the trunk," a gruff voice said.

The sound of footsteps echoed through the near-empty garage. She willed her body to work faster at getting rid of the drug. Once she was in the trunk of some car or they decide to pump more drugs into her, it might be harder to escape.

"What's taking him so long? We gotta—what the fuck? You guys secured this place, right?"

"Yeah, boss, we did."

"What the—motherfucker! Take care of him!"

The grip on her tightened and she felt her kidnapper swing around and then run. She lifted her head, struggling to focus her vision as her head bobbed up and down as they sped away.

There were three blurry figures behind her. One

moved around fast and then two fell to the ground. The man carrying her faltered in his steps, making her bump her nose into his back. When she looked up again, she saw it. A flash of silver running straight for her.

Darius.

He sped up and caught up with them, grabbing her arms and pulling her from her abductor. She wrapped her arms around his neck and they tumbled to the ground.

"Run, Adrianna!" he urged as he scrambled to his feet. "Get away from here."

He turned around to face the man coming after them. As her vision focused, she saw something metallic in the other man's hand. A gun.

"No!" she screamed. Darius lunged for the man, and his body jerked as three gunshots echoed through the garage. Her inner wolf howled, and she struggled to control it while getting to her feet. As she stumbled towards them, she heard a fourth gunshot.

"Oh, God!" Darius was lying down on the cement floor on his back, his shirt stained with red. The other man was a few feet away, facedown and unmoving, blood beginning to seep out from under his body. "Darius! Darius, please!" She knelt down and cradled his face in her hands. "Please be okay! Don't die!"

His eyelids flew open, and he gave her a weak grin. "I won't." To her horror, he let out a sick gurgle and spat out some blood. "The bullets went through. My body will heal in no time."

She knew he was right; he was a Lycan after all and the

wounds were probably starting to close already. It didn't stop that pit in the bottom of her stomach from forming. "I should get some help. I can call—"

"No!" His hand grasped at the lapel of her jacket. "No. I'm fine. We should go. I can't be found here like this."

She hesitated but realized that if they got the authorities involved, it would be terribly messy. They could cause trouble for the Virginia clan, and the senator would not like that. "I have a suite. We can go there." She hooked her arms under his chest. "Can you make it up the stairs?"

"I can," he said.

He was heavy, but she was a Lycan too. She could carry him up bridal-style, but he would probably protest. The walk up twelve flights of stairs wouldn't be good for his wounds, but using the elevators were too risky.

They were nearing the staircase entrance when a loud screech made them both look behind. Loud shouts and curses came from the direction of where they had left her kidnapper bleeding out on the ground, followed by the sound of a car door slamming and then an engine roaring away.

"Do you think they escaped?" she asked.

"Perhaps." He gritted his teeth. "They should pay for what they tried to do but—" He let out a hiss and clutched at the wound.

"We'll take care of that later," she said. "Take a deep breath. It's a long trip up."

The climb up to her suite was slow and daunting as Darius struggled with his wounds. He tried to keep his face neutral, but she could see that he was in a lot of pain. She nearly cried with relief when they reached the top floor, and she quickly got him into her suite.

"I'm all right," he said as he disentangled himself from her.

"You're still bleeding," she pointed out. "C'mon." She grabbed his hand and pulled him into the bedroom.

He grimaced when he looked at the pristine King-sized bed. "I'll ruin the sheets."

"That doesn't matter. *Ay basta*! Stop being such stubborn man!" She practically pushed him down on top of the covers. Reaching for the bottom of his shirt, she lifted up the fabric gingerly. "Ugh. That's nasty. But," she peered at the two holes on his abdomen, "it looks like it's stopped bleeding. Take that shirt off, and I'll get some towels to clean you up."

She headed into the bathroom and twisted the tap in the sink on, then ran two hand towels under the water. When she came back to the bedroom, Darius had his eyes closed and his breathing was even. *Good.* Sleep would help the healing process.

Just as she'd predicted, the wounds had stopped bleeding. His flesh was knitting itself back together, but the skin hadn't regenerated yet. *Gross.* She cleaned up around the lesions, wiping the blood and dirt from his skin. It would be a few hours before he was fully recovered, but at least he wasn't going to die.

As soon as she was done, she went back to the bathroom and tossed the towels into a plastic laundry bag, giving herself a mental note to throw them into the garbage before she went to work. Her blouse and suit were ruined, so those went into the bag too.

She stepped into the shower and twisted the tap on to the hottest setting she could stand. It felt good, the water washing over her and cleaning off the remaining blood that clung to her skin.

God, this was an awful day. First the explosion, then the kidnapping. She didn't even want to think about who those men were. She was exhausted beyond belief. The only bright part was that Darius was here and he was going to be all right. She didn't even care about what happened yesterday. He survived, just like he said he would. That was all that mattered.

When she was done, she wrapped herself in a robe and headed back into the bedroom. She stopped when she heard voices.

"Darius? Darius!"

His eyes were still closed, but his mouth was moving. "Ta ... Ma ... Thoms ... Elena!" Arms reached out, then dropped down to his side as his body tensed. His face twisted in agony, and he let out a pained moan.

He was dreaming. But what should she do? Wasn't it bad to wake up someone who was having a nightmare? Or was that sleepwalking?

His breathing was deep and heaving, and she reached out to touch his chest. If he moved around too much, it would set back the healing process. His muscles jumped under her touch, but then he settled back into the pillows.

He was talking again, but she couldn't understand half the words. It sounded like he was pleading, and the agony in his voice made her heart clench. She climbed into bed next to him and lay her head on his shoulder. "Darius," she whispered, pressing her lips to his warm skin. "It's going to be okay."

What was he dreaming about? And who was Elena? So many questions ran through her head. But the adrenaline was leaving her body, leaving exhaustion to take over. *I'll just close my eyes for a bit*, she told herself.

CHAPTER FIFTEEN

Darius had recovered from many injuries in the past, from cuts and abrasions from fights to knife and gunshot wounds that had hit major arteries. However, he had to admit that waking up as his body healed had never been quite as pleasant as it was now.

Adrianna's head was on his shoulder and an arm thrown over his chest. He could feel her steady breath against his skin as her parted lips were pressed up against his bicep. Her hair was splayed down her back like a mahogany carpet while the robe she wore had parted sometime during the night and her bare breasts were pushed against his arm. He reached over and lifted a lock of hair that had fallen over her beautiful face, brushing the smooth skin of her cheek.

He glanced down and saw that the wounds on his stomach had closed up. The skin was still pink and the skin webbed, but it wasn't even swollen. Slowly, he turned to his side so he could cradle her body. Her eyelids fluttered, and by the time she opened them to reveal her mismatched eyes, he had fully enveloped her in his arms.

"Is it morning?" she asked sleepily.

"No, it's not even dawn." He held her tighter, hoping she wouldn't try to get up. He just wanted to feel her like this for now. And maybe longer.

"I can't believe you came," she whispered. "It was a good thing too. I guess my parents weren't being overly cautious. The mages must have someone keeping tabs on me and they knew that I was alone."

She had already come to the conclusion that it was the mages that came after her. Of course, he didn't know for sure if Anatoli was behind the attempt to kidnap her. Or if Mila had been telling the truth at all. If he didn't say anything or contradict her, he wasn't lying. At least that's what he told himself.

"I told you I would protect you, Adrianna." He stroked the side of her face with his fingers. "And that you didn't have to worry about me."

"That you did." She didn't move or flinch away from his touch. "I should tell my mother—"

He tightened his grip. "It's early, no one will be up yet. It can wait until later."

"I suppose ..."

"Sleep, *lupoaică,*" he urged. "You still have a lot to deal with when you wake."

She relaxed against him and sighed. He was wide awake, and he figured he could use this time to think of what to do tomorrow. Maybe he could track down those men who tried to kidnap Adrianna and get some information. Or go back and find out what Anatoli was up to. Or maybe—

"Darius?" She squirmed away from him, then lifted her head to look him in the eyes.

"Yes?"

"Who's Elena?"

His muscles tensed up at the sound of the name. The involuntary response didn't escape her notice and her eyes widened.

"How do you know that name?"

"Um, from you. You were saying it in your sleep." Her brows scrunched together. "And other things too. Ta ... ma? And Thom?"

"*Mama,* you know the meaning as it is the same in English, but *Tată* is Romanian for father." He rolled onto his back, releasing her from his embrace. "Thomsin and Elena were my brother and sister."

"Were?" He saw her flinch visibly. "Oh. I'm sorry. I shouldn't have brought it up." She inched back, shrinking with dejection as she curled away from him.

He let out a sigh and faced her. "It was a long time ago."

Mismatched eyes blinked up at him. "What happened to them?"

"I don't know."

"You ... don't know? Did they just disappear?"

"They died, all of them, but I don't know how." He

paused, debating with himself if he should go on. Maybe it was better she knew now. So she knew what she was dealing with if she chose to continue this path they were on.

But where would he begin? From the start, he supposed. "We lived in a Lycan settlement village in Romania. One day, my father got a letter from a man claiming to be his father. Gregor Corvinus. He had apparently gotten my grandmother pregnant and left her behind to start a new life in America with his wife and his son. He invited my father to come to New Jersey and be part of The Family. We were poor and barely surviving, so he went so he could make a better life for us."

"Oh, Darius." She moved closer and took his hand in hers.

"I was nine when he left, Thomsin was five, and Elena was just a baby. He was gone for five years but would send us every cent he made and letters almost every week. One day, we got the letter my mother had been waiting for. He was sending for us, and we would be living in New Jersey with him." He remembered Mama's excitement as she clutched the letter to her breast. "So, we packed up what little belongings we had and made our way to America. I was fourteen." That journey was so clear in his mind. The fear. The anticipation. The elation that they would all be together again. "We got here and well, it was just as my father had said. Our grandfather—his father—doted on us. We lived in a nice home—not a mansion, but it didn't have dirt floors—and my siblings and I went to school and wore new clothes. Then one day—"

The lump in his throat made him stop. She squeezed his hand and he felt the tightness in his ribcage ease. "I was sitting in the kitchen doing my homework. My parents where there and Elena was sitting in her high chair. Thomsin was on the floor, playing with his toys. That was the last thing I remember. Next thing I knew, I was in the hospital."

"What?" she said in an incredulous voice. "That's it? But your family—"

"Was dead. That's what my Grandfather told me when I woke up. My mother on the floor. Father a few feet from her. Elena and Thomsin ... none of them had any injuries, and there was no evidence of foul play. Grandfather was heartbroken and he died soon after because of grief."

"Darius, I'm so sorry," her voice choked up, and she scrambled to his side, pressing her nose to his shoulder.

"Do not cry, Adrianna," he said when he felt the wetness from her face. "I told you, it was a long time ago."

She sniffed. "And no one knew what caused their deaths?"

"They didn't find anything conclusive. It was like ... their hearts just stopped. The private investigator my grandfather hired said it might have been some unknown chemical from a nearby plant."

"But you survived unscathed?"

He ran his hand through his hair. "Not quite. My hair

turned this color permanently. Which is why the PI thought it might have been chemical related." To this day, however, he still hadn't found any substance that changed hair color permanently. He had tried to find out more about his family's death, but was met with the same dead ends as the private investigator.

"Darius ... I'm so sorry." She reached up and ran her fingers through his hair, massaging his scalp. "I'm so sorry."

"Don't." He grabbed her hand gently. "Do not pity me."

Her mouth opened in shock. "I didn't ... this isn't pity." She lifted her head to meet his gaze. "You're so strong, going through all that and still coming out on the other side."

He came out alive, but he had been changed permanently. His wolf had changed, too. He had just learned to shift that summer before they left, but after that, it became unmanageable. He would black out at random times, waking up and realizing that he had shifted and his wolf took total control of their body. Anatoli had him locked up for weeks until he went back to normal. At least, learned to make it seem like he was normal. "I should have died with them. I shouldn't have survived."

"No!" She wrapped her arms tight around him. "I won't have you saying such things. You were a boy. Maybe you were meant to survive."

"We will never know," he said.

"I'm sorry you lost your family," she said in a quiet

voice. "I feel terrible though. You wouldn't be hurt if it wasn't for me."

"I would gladly be hurt a hundred times if it meant I could hold you like this. Every moment spent with you is worth any pain." The confession came out of nowhere but he was glad he said it. Letting her think that he only wanted her body and didn't care for her at all had been eating away at him.

"Are you feeling better?" Her hands ran over his stomach. "All healed up?"

"Yes. I'm feeling fine—" He stopped short when she slid her body over him, straddling his hips. "Adrianna?"

"My choice." She slid the robe off her shoulders, baring herself to him. "This is my choice."

He let out a grunt when she placed her hands on his abs and trailed her fingers up his chest, leaning down so she could press her lips to his for a slow, thoughtful kiss. God, she was sweeter than honey, than anything else he'd ever tasted.

Spreading her legs wider, she rocked her hips against him and mewled against his mouth. He grabbed the robe and pulled it off completely, leaving her naked. Her arousal perfumed the air, and he groaned as he could feel the heat of her core on his cock even through his jeans and underwear.

A surprised gasp escaped her lips when he flipped her over. Impatiently, he unbuttoned his fly and tugged his jeans down over his hips. His cock was fully hard and aching to be in her. But he wanted to feast on her delectable, curvy body first. He kissed her hard again, then trailed kisses lower, down to her bare breasts.

"Darius!" Her fingers grabbed at his hair when he took a nipple into his mouth. He sucked in deep as his other hand teased and pinched the other. A soft nip with his teeth had her squirming beneath him.

"Please," she begged. "I need you. Inside me."

"Not yet," he whispered. "Just let me have another taste." He moved lower, nipping and sucking at her delicate skin. When his head was between her thighs, he took in a deep breath, drowning in the scent of her. He pressed his mouth to her sex, spreading her juices all over with his tongue and lips. She bucked her hips at him, and he slid his tongue inside her tight pussy. God, she would feel incredible around his cock. He reached down to stroke himself to ease the ache while continuing to lave her with his tongue.

"Darius!" she cried out when his mouth found her clit. The bud was swollen and begging for his attention. He lashed at it with his tongue and she sobbed as her body shook with pleasure, her hands digging into his shoulders.

"Adrianna." He shrugged his remaining clothes off, then pushed her knees apart as he positioned himself to take her. "I want you so bad." Guiding his shaft, he pressed the tip of his cock against her entrance.

Her hands clung to his shoulders, her fingers like claws digging into his flesh as he began to move. She was so tight and warm, and even though her pussy was drenched, she still winced as he filled her.

"God. Adrianna. You're so—*ungh*!" She squeezed

around him and he thought he would lose it. He wasn't ready yet. Wanted to give her pleasure. Make her moan. Make her scream his name.

He pulled her hair to force her head back, and he swooped down to give her a deep kiss. It was rough and wild, but she didn't protest, instead moaned against his mouth. His tongue slipped into her mouth and he moved his hips to match the rhythm.

The feel of her around him was unlike anything he'd ever experienced before. Her lush body, her lips, her entire being was swallowing him whole, and he didn't want it to stop.

He hooked his arms under her legs, then pulled her lower on the bed so he could put his feet on the ground for more leverage. She let out a loud yelp as he thrust hard into her, and her eyeballs rolled back.

"Oh God! Oh God!"

Her breasts bounced deliciously with each thrust, and when he changed the angle of his hips, she screamed his name and fisted her hands into the sheets above her. Wrapping her legs around his waist, he loomed over her, grabbing her wrists and pinning her to the bed so he could lean down and devour her succulent lips again.

She squeezed hard around him, pulsing around his cock as she orgasmed again. He let her ride it out, peaking and then bringing her down before slamming hard into her, pummeling into her furiously, demanding another orgasm from her. He didn't stop until her body was shaking and she let out a pleasured whimper.

"Please, Darius," she sobbed. "I can't possibly come anymore ..."

"No," he growled. "You'll be done when I say you are."

He lifted her up and then bounced her body, impaling her on his cock. She clung to him, her hips pistoning up and down on him until her tight pussy pulsed around him and he felt her juices run down his cock and drench his thighs. He turned around and sat down on the bed so she straddled him.

"Move," he ordered.

She obeyed, grinding her hips against his. Reaching down between them, he found her swollen clit and gave it a soft pinch. That sent her over the edge and he could feel her tightening around him again. He pumped his hips up at her, meeting her thrusts and when he felt that now-familiar fluttering of her pussy, he let go, roaring loudly as his cock pulsed and twitched and filled her with his seed. It felt like it went on forever, his heart racing and the blood pumping in his veins as pleasure coursed through him.

He felt physically and mentally drained, so he fell back on the bed. Adrianna collapsed on top of him, her breath coming in gasps. He stroked her back until her breathing evened, and he felt his cock go soft and slip out of her.

Neither moved for a few heartbeats, but eventually, she lifted her head up. "I should get ready."

He checked the clock on the bedside table. "You can wait a few more minutes."

"I—Darius!" She giggled when he rolled her over and

pinned her down on the bed. "Don't think this will stop me from getting out of bed."

"I'm stronger than you," he teased. She looked even more beautiful with the afterglow of their lovemaking clearly marked on her face.

"I wish I didn't have to. I could stay in here with you all day."

"Why don't you?"

Her brows knitted together. "You know why. I still have this crisis to deal with."

The explosion at the restaurant. He'd lost his mind and forgotten why she was here. "You have an entire suite outside," he said. "Couldn't you work from here? I promise to stay inside the bedroom." He nipped at her lips. "Besides, you're dealing with a lot today and you'll surely be stressed out. And I know a great way to relieve your tensions."

"Do you, now? I—*Ooohhh*, Darius!" she purred as he kissed her neck, dragging his lips along the delicate column. "I guess that's not a bad idea."

"It's a fantastic idea."

CHAPTER SIXTEEN

Staying in her suite was, indeed, a fantastic idea. For one thing, she had more privacy and she didn't have to feel like a goldfish in a bowl while she sat in Emerson Communications' meeting room. But, having Darius nearby actually helped her focus on her work and do what she needed to do to manage this crisis. His presence was soothing, even though he was just sitting on the couch a few feet away from her. Plus, as he said, he was able to help her relieve her stress. Three times.

Heat crept into her cheeks, thinking about all the sex in the last twelve hours. Even in her past relationships, it was never like this. She wondered if it was because Darius was a Lycan that she seemed extra frisky around him. And God, that *body*. He seemed amused that she found his rock-hard abs and muscled chest so attractive that she had to order him to put on a robe or else she wasn't going to get any work done.

Speaking of work, it seemed like the crisis was mostly handled, though she still had to make a live appearance on a cable news network show tomorrow morning to reassure people that it was safe to go to their restaurants. Now that she had time to breathe, it was time to call her mother and tell her about what happened last night. It shouldn't be a difficult call, but as a grown woman, it was still hard to concede to her parents that they were right all along.

"*Mimma*, how's everything?" Frankie said as soon as she picked up.

"As well as it could be," she said before rattling off the list of things she had accomplished, including setting up a trust for the families of those who had died in the accident.

"Excellent, I knew you could handle it." The fierce pride in her mother's voice was evident. "Now, is there anything else?"

She took a long, deep breath. "Yes." She already knew how Frankie would react to the fact that she had waited a whole day to tell her that she was almost kidnapped. It didn't make the ear-blasting she got sting less.

When Frankie finally calmed down, she said, "I'm so relieved you're safe, Adrianna. And now I'm glad I followed my instincts and agreed to have Darius guard you."

"Yeah, Mama, me too." She glanced over at Darius, who was sitting on the couch, watching the muted TV. His robe had opened into a deep V, showing off his tattoos and those muscled pecs she enjoyed kissing and biting. Her eyes trailed down to the tantalizing view of his abs and the trail of hair that disappeared under the robe. He must have felt her stare because he turned his head, his cobalt eyes sending her a look that made her core clench.

"Adrianna? Adrianna? Are you there?"

"Yes! I'm here. I mean—" She crossed her legs, hoping that would ease the ache. "Was there anything else?"

"I think we're good. I'm coming home the day after tomorrow," she said. "And I have a surprise for you."

"A surprise?"

"Yes, but I'm still arranging it. I'll tell you once I'm back."

"All right, Mama, I'll talk to you then. Say hello to Uncle Dante."

"I will. You be careful. Bye, *mimma*."

When she heard the soft click of the receiver and the line went dead, she put the phone down on the table.

"Everything okay?" Darius's hand landed gently on her back, making soothing circles.

"Yes. Actually, it went better than I thought," she chuckled. "I half expected her to send an army down here."

"You do not need an army. All you need is me."

Do I ever.

"I've ordered dinner from room service," he said. "I didn't know what you wanted, so I ordered one of everything from the menu."

Her stomach gurgled loudly at the thought of food.

"Oh good, I'm starving." Going through a PR crises must burn thousands of calories because she had eaten enough food for ten men today. Or maybe it was the sex ...

He took her hand and pulled her up. "It's past seven, and you've been working all day."

"Well, not *all* day," she teased. "So, what time will room service be here?"

"Twenty minutes?"

"So, what you're saying is, we have time?"

He tugged the robe off his shoulders and let it fall to the floor.

Oh, madre de dio.

Shower sex had never been on her bucket list; in fact, it sounded uncomfortable and not enjoyable at all. But, as her body wracked with a second orgasm from Darius's furious pounding into her while holding her against the wet tiles of her bathroom en suite, she was glad she'd experienced it before she left this earth, as well as the other pleasures he'd introduced her to for the last two days.

"Please, Darius, no more," she whimpered, the spray of the rainfall shower blinding her vision.

"One more, Adrianna," he said in between thrusts. "One more for me."

She screamed his name, her voice echoing and bouncing off the walls. He captured her mouth to silence her, his mouth devouring hers as he pummeled harder into her, grunting as she felt his cock spasm, his warm, sticky come pumping into her.

When the pounding of her heartbeat slowed down—or was that his?—she unhooked her legs from him. He pulled out of her and set her down gently on the floor. "You did great." He kissed the top of her head.

"Uh, thanks?" She gave him a teasing smile. "I'm going to feel that though," she said, wincing as she tried to take a step forward. "I'm going to feel all of it."

"You did not protest when I woke you up this morning," he said. "Or late last night. Or that time before dinner. Or after room service left."

"You've made your point," she said with a laugh. "We should—" The sound of the doorbell interrupted her.

"Are you expecting anyone?"

"No." It was early in the morning and the car wasn't picking her up to take her to the TV station until later that day. "I should go check who it is." She grabbed her robe as she exited the stall and headed out into the main suite.

"All right, all right! Hold your horses!" The bell continued to ring impatiently and she picked up her pace. She yanked the door open. "What the hell is the matter—Julianna? What are you doing here?"

Her sister stood on the other side of the door, hands on her hips, a frown creasing her forehead. "I've been calling you since I got into the city," she said. "And I sent you a message this morning about me coming here. Didn't you get it?"

"Uh ..." She didn't get to check her phone first thing

this morning, as waking up with Darius's head between her legs had proven to be a distraction. "Sorry. I've been busy."

Julianna stepped past her and made her way into the suite. "Mama called last night and asked that I come here. Why didn't you tell me someone tried to kidnap you? Or that Darius apparently showed up here and—" She stopped suddenly, her eyes narrowing.

"Julianna?"

She glanced around, as if looking for something.

"Julianna, wait!"

But her sister had already dashed toward the bedroom. She cursed loudly as she tried to catch her before she got to the door. "Wait, I—"

Julianna's eyes were as big as frisbees, and understandably so, seeing as Darius came out of the bathroom wearing only a towel around his waist. She looked at the rumpled sheets on the bed, then at Darius, then back at Adrianna.

"I can explain," she began.

"If it didn't stink of sex in here, I might have eaten up any lie you would have told me because I can't believe you would do this!" Julianna raged, the fury in her voice barely contained.

"I wasn't going to lie." She looked to Darius helplessly.

"It's not what you think," he began. "We are—"

"I'd like to speak to my sister alone, please," Julianna said, not even looking at him.

He flashed Adrianna a concerned look, but she nodded.

"Of course," he said. "I'll be outside." He grabbed his discarded pants from the floor and headed outside.

Darius was barely out of earshot when Julianna started raving. "What. The. Hell!" she cried. "I can't believe you're fucking him! Is this some form of Stockholm syndrome where—"

"He's not keeping me hostage," she retorted. "And I know what I'm doing!"

"Know what you're—" Julianna raised her hands in frustration. "Something's not right with that guy! I know it." There was a dangerous glint in her eyes. "He can't stay here."

"He's here to protect me! Or don't you remember Mama's orders?"

"I mean," Julianna began, "he can't stay here *in D.C.*" She put her hands on her hips. "Tell me, when you spoke to Mama did you conveniently leave out the part where he didn't have permission from Senator Burns to be in this territory?"

Dammit! She knew she should have secured permission from the Alpha as soon as Darius got here, but she had been too distracted. "You wouldn't dare."

"Try me."

She spun around, unable to stay in the same room with her sister at that moment. Marching out the door, she found Darius standing by the bedroom door.

"She's right," he said. "We have waited too long to ask for permission."

"I could still ask him."

"But there will be a price to pay," he said. "And you know how politicians are."

"True, but it would be worth it. I don't want to be apart from you."

"Be practical," he said, placing a hand on her shoulder. "You're headed back to Jersey tomorrow, right?"

"Yeah."

"If I leave now, no one will know I'd ever been here," he said. "Julianna will be able to protect you until then. Besides, I must drive my car back anyway."

"I—" She knew he was right. It would be childish, not to mention risky, to let him stay here, even if Julianna didn't threaten to rat him out. "Fine."

"I'll be at your house when you arrive. I promise." He wrapped his arms around her waist, pulled her close, and smothered her lips with urgent fervor.

As usual, his kisses left her breathless. "I'll hold you to that."

"I know you will."

As he turned to leave, she grabbed his hand. "Wait."

"Yes?"

"Remember what I said." She squeezed his palm. "This was *my* choice."

Surprise flashed across his face, then he lifted her hand to his lips. "Stay safe."

When the door closed behind him, an ache began to form in her chest. Her she-wolf, which had been calm and contented these past twenty-four hours, began to whine with grief.

Mine. Mine.

She started at the voice. *No, I must have imagined it.* Shaking her head, she took a deep breath and mentally prepared herself to deal with her sister.

CHAPTER SEVENTEEN

Leaving Adrianna was difficult, to the point of painful. For one thing, he felt *literal* pain as his wolf was ripping him up from the inside, enraged that they would leave her so vulnerable like that. He reasoned that he was doing this for her own good, as he had no idea if Julianna would make good on her threat. Breaking territorial boundaries held severe punishments, and if the Alpha of this territory found out, there would be consequences for him and Adrianna.

His wolf didn't understand politics or rules, of course, and so he bore the pain as he drove back to New Jersey, only taking comfort in the fact that Adrianna would be safe with her sister.

Besides, he had more pressing matters to attend to. The sooner he found out the truth from Anatoli—hopefully, that he had not orchestrated the kidnapping—the sooner he could be back with his she-wolf again.

Making love to Adrianna was better than any wildest fantasy he ever had. She was passionate but also unselfish. So eager to please him in any way. Even now, thoughts of her soft, plush body underneath his made him hard as steel. The thoughts of what other delicious things he would do to her–and her to him–made the long drive home both pleasurable and torturous.

When he saw the gate of the compound ahead of him, he began to mentally prepare himself for the confrontation with Anatoli. He needed to be smart about this as accusing his uncle of such a crime if he were innocent would not be without its consequences. Alternately, if Anatoli was responsible, then there were bigger things to worry about.

The gates opened for him, and he hadn't even entered the garage when he saw two other enforcers already waiting for him. He recognized them as Remus and Simion, two of Anatoli's meanest men, as well as his most loyal. They stopped him and motioned for him to get out of the car.

"Your uncle has instructed us to take you to him as soon as you arrived." Remus attempted to grab his arm, but he sent the man a scathing look that had him faltering.

"He's waiting," Simion added but didn't make a move toward him.

So, Anatoli already knew he was on the way. Whether that was good or bad, well ... he would find out soon enough.

The moment he entered Anatoli's office, the old man came at him with blinding rage. Remus and Simion held his arms back as a meaty fist connected with his jaw. "I should have you whipped!" Anatoli screamed. "Then wait for you to heal and then whip you again!"

Even when his arms were set free, he refused to cower or even wipe the blood that dripped from his lip. He was used to this. After all, when Anatoli took over for Grandfather as head of The Family, he used terror and abuse to keep everyone in line. "Why should I be punished, Uncle?"

"For foiling my plans! When those humans I had sent after Adrianna Anderson told me they were stopped by a silver-haired devil, I knew it was you!"

"You ordered me to be her bodyguard. I was only doing as you asked."

That seemed to infuriate him even more and his face went red. "That's not ... insolent boy!" The back of his hand whipped against his cheekbone. "I—I was told she went to D.C. alone. I thought maybe she'd become annoyed with you and dismissed you. Besides, according to Mila, you've found out nothing useful these past days!"

"Why do you want to harm the Alpha's daughter?"

"None of your business!" He cracked his knuckles, then his lips spread into a smile. "However, while your actions thwarted my plans for that bitch, you've actually made things better."

Better? What did his uncle mean? "How so?"

"I received a call from the Alpha herself. Frankie Anderson was incredibly grateful that you were there to rescue her daughter." He let out a cackle. "What a stupid whore!" He signaled at the two enforcers to leave, and once they did, he gave Darius a pat on the shoulders. "Now, they will be easier to manipulate. You will remain by that bitch's side and keep gaining her trust. Then," he licked his lips, "once the time comes, I will tell you what to do."

Darius swallowed hard. The sick bastard hurt him for no reason other than to show his dominance around his minions, but worse than that, he was now trapped. It would be too late to confess to Adrianna that he suspected it was Anatoli who sent those men to kidnap her, but at this point, neither could he betray his uncle without tipping him off or protecting her.

"Do you understand me, Darius?" Anatoli looked him straight in the eyes. "The Family comes first."

"Of course."

"Good. That's exactly the attitude I need."

The only way out of this would be to find out what Anatoli was really planning and put a stop to it, without him knowing any better. This was obviously more than just keeping The Family's interests in the territory. His uncle wouldn't go to such lengths or risk death by attempting to harm a future Alpha. But that would mean playing both sides, and he knew now that he could never let anything happen to Adrianna.

He could only hope to find out the truth before she did.

CHAPTER EIGHTEEN

"So, do you think Zac and Astrid are going to have a girl or boy?"

Julianna looked up at her from her phone, raised a brow, and went back to tapping on her screen.

"I think a girl would be nice," Adrianna added. "Maybe she'll be sassy like her mom and grandma. Though a boy would probably make Nick Vrost go over the moon."

No response.

"Or maybe they'll have a monkey. A cute little chimp with a furry face."

When that didn't elicit a response from her sister, she threw her hands up. "It's been over a day, Julianna. Are you really going to not talk to me?"

All she got was a freezing stare.

Seeing as Julianna was determined to keep giving her the silent treatment, she instead looked outside the windows watching the clouds as their private plane flew through the skies on their way to New Jersey. She had hoped that Julianna's silent fury would lessen especially since Darius wasn't around anymore, but she was wrong. Her sister only seemed determined to ignore her as way to show her displeasure.

I'm a grown woman. She could sleep with whomever she wanted, whenever she wanted. Besides, she really didn't know what was bothering Julianna. Maybe her sister needed to get laid. If she could find someone who was half as good in bed as Darius was, maybe she wouldn't be such a sourpuss.

Of course, thinking of Darius in bed only made her remember the mind-blowing sex they had, and her core throbbed with excitement, knowing that he was waiting for her at home. Hopefully, Julianna would have cooled off by then, though she wasn't sure how much privacy she and Darius would have with her just down the hall in Uncle Dante's old room.

"Excuse me, Ms. Anderson," Steve, their steward on the plane said as he approached them. "We'll be landing shortly."

"Thank you."

She was glad they were almost there as anticipation throbbed in her veins. God, she never thought she'd be the type to go crazy over a man, but it seems she'd found her weakness in Darius. Just thinking of his devilish tongue and his hands made her giddy with anticipation.

The jet had barely stopped on the tarmac when

Julianna unbuckled her seatbelt and reached for her bag in the overhead bin.

"Where are you going?" she asked her sister.

"I have stuff to do in New York," Julianna replied in a clipped voice. "Uncle Nick arranged for someone to bring you home." Slinging her duffel over her shoulder, she marched toward the door, tapping her foot impatiently. The moment it swung open, she disappeared without even waving goodbye or a glance back.

She hated having Julianna so angry at her, but at the same time, her sister was being unreasonable. Maybe someday, she'd understand if she ever had a boyfriend.

Boyfriend?

She felt her cheeks go hot. Calling Darius that seemed trite. Beau? Lover? Oh dear. She couldn't see herself introducing him that way. Wait, how was she going to introduce him to other people? And then there was the rest of her family.

"Ms. Anderson? Is there anything else I can do for you?" Steve asked as he stood next to her.

"Oh." Embarrassed at being caught daydreaming, she quickly got to her feet. "No, I'm fine. Thank you, Steve."

"It was a pleasure to have you on board, as always."

She grabbed her purse and allowed Steve to help her put her coat on before she walked out of the plane. Who could Nick have sent to bring her home, she wondered? As she descended the stairs, she saw who it was and smiled.

"Adrianna!" Astrid Jonasson—now Vrost—greeted, waving her hands excitedly.

"Astrid!" She nearly tripped down the stairs in her hurry to get to her friend. The warm embrace that greeted her made her want to weep with relief. She and the younger woman had gotten along very well the last time she was assigned to be her protector.

"Nice to see you too," Astrid laughed. "Are you okay? Was the flight good? Is Steve the steward still hot?"

She chuckled. "Yes, yes, and yes!" She squeezed her tighter. "I'm so glad to see you." And Astrid didn't even know the half of it.

"Me too!"

"And I have to say, I'm honored that the future Beta of New York is the one protecting me today." After the mages attacked them at the ball, Lucas had declared that he wanted Astrid to be his Beta, much to everyone's surprise. Astrid, after all, was not even a full-fledged member of the Lycan Security Team. However, she did prove her worth by saving Lucas which only endeared the young woman to Adrianna more.

Astrid gave her a strange look. "Say, you look ... different?"

"Different?"

"Yeah ... it's like ..." She leaned in. "Are you using a new skin cream? Or maybe shampoo?"

"Huh? No. I've only been using my usual stuff."

"Weird." She sniffed at her. "It's like ... I don't know. Never mind. C'mon, let's go." She gestured to the black SUV behind her. She followed Astrid into the car and hopped in behind her friend. Astrid gave instructions to the driver, and soon they were off.

"So, I can't believe Uncle Nick sent you," Adrianna began. "I mean, I'm glad he did, but you would think he and Zac would have you wrapped up in blankets while atop ten mattresses until the baby comes."

"Me, nah!" Astrid rubbed the non-existent bump on her belly. "Besides, this is a True Mates baby. As you know, nothing can harm me, which is why he sent me to come get you." She picked up a large paper bag from the back. "I heard about your kidnapping attempt. If anyone tries to get to you, they'll have to go through me first."

"Well I'm glad—" She stopped when Astrid opened the bag and the scent of dough and sugar hit her nostrils. "Oh," she groaned. "That smells amazing. What is it?"

"These?" Astrid reached inside and took something out the size of a baseball. "Freshly made donuts. I got them on the way here." She took a big bite and swallowed it in one gulp. "I swear, this baby is driving me crazy, always demanding food."

Her mouth began to water and her stomach made a loud noise. "Er, sorry."

"No worries." She offered the bag to her. "Want one?"

She nearly tore into the paper grabbing a donut. It was still warm and soft, and she shoved it into her mouth, devouring the whole thing in two bites. "*Rmmrhhmmm* ... good." She wiped her mouth with the napkin Astrid held out to her. "Sorry, it was really delicious." It was strange though, as she just ate on the plane. In fact, she had devoured the burger and fries Steve had prepared for her.

"Don't worry," she said. "Want more?"

She and Astrid polished off the dozen donuts she bought, and finally she felt satisfied. She was also glad for the her presence, as being in the company of the vivacious young woman who told her hilarious stories kept her entertained throughout the ride.

"We're here," Astrid said. "Ooh, your house is gorgeous."

"You've never been here, right?" she said. "I can take you on a tour. And maybe we can grab dinner at Muccino's."

"That sounds awesome, but," the younger woman shook her head, "I'm actually just supposed to drop you off and keep an eye on you until you got home."

"Oh."

"Yeah, sorry, I'd love to hang out, though it looks like you won't be all alone."

She turned her head toward the window, expecting Darius to be standing on the porch, waiting for her as he said, or even a glimpse of his gray Dodge Charger. To her disappointment, she only saw a black town car in the driveway and four burly men in dark suits on the porch.

"Who are those men?" she asked Astrid. She recognized two of them as part of the New York Lycan Security Team, but not the other two. "Did you have a new batch of recruits graduate from training?"

Astrid wrinkled her nose. "I don't—oh!" She snapped

her fingers. "I think those are the security guys for your mom's VIP guest."

"Guest?"

"Yeah, hush-hush security team confidential secret stuff," she said with a grin. "Nick's been including me in the daily briefings as part of my training. Anyway, you should head inside. Then I can say I completed my first solo assignment as future Beta of New York with success."

"Er, okay." She supposed she'd find out soon enough who this guest was. "It really was nice seeing you, Astrid. I know I live out of the way now, but please come see me anytime. I'll treat you to as much food as you want at the restaurant."

Astrid chuckled. "I will, but you may regret that promise."

She waved goodbye to Astrid then headed into the house. The two guards from the New York team immediately recognized her and rushed to open the door to the front. When she went inside, she followed the sounds of rapid-fire Italian all the way into the living room. Frankie was sitting on the couch, talking to someone sitting on the armchair whose back was turned to her. When her mother realized she was standing in the doorway, her face lit up.

"*Mimma!*" Frankie got to her feet and bolted to her side. "I'm so glad to see you!" She embraced her daughter tight. "I was so scared when you told me what happened."

"I'm fine, Mama," she said. "Don't worry about me."

She wiped the tears at the corner of her eyes. "Of

course I'll worry about you. You're my daughter. I'm just happy Darius was there to save you."

"Yeah." Speaking of which, where was Darius? He promised he would be here when she arrived. "Have you seen him, by the way?"

"Darius? I thought he was with you?"

So, Julianna hadn't said anything to their mother. *Yet.* "Um, you know he couldn't stay for too long. Not without permission. He left when Julianna came."

"Good thinking," Frankie said. "Oh, dear. I'm being rude to our guest." She turned around. "*Perdonami, scusami tanto,* Alesso."

The man who had been sitting on the armchair rose, and now she saw his face. "It's quite all right, Francesca." So, this was her mother's guest. The man looked to be about her age, handsome with dark blond hair and hazel eyes. He gave her a warm smile.

"May I introduce my daughter and my heir, Adrianna Callista Anderson. Adrianna, this is Count Alesso di Cavour, Alpha of Rome."

"How do you do?" she greeted politely and extended her hand. "You honor us with your presence, Alpha. It's my pleasure to welcome you to New Jersey." Actually, she was blindsided by his visit, but she gave him the standard polite greeting when welcoming a visiting Alpha.

"The pleasure is all mine." He took her hand and lifted it to his lips. "I've heard so much about you, Adrianna."

I bet you have, she thought as she gave her mother a

sideways glance. "What brings you to our territory, Count Alesso?"

"Please, just Alesso," he insisted as he finally let go of her hand. "Your mother and uncle were in Rome and they invited me for a visit. I have never been to New Jersey."

"I'm sure you'll find it riveting," she said dryly.

"I've asked Alesso to come so we can have a discussion about future alliances," Frankie said. "Since we have such close heritages, it's a shame we never had any close ties."

"My uncle said you broke his heart when you married Grant Anderson," Alesso quipped. "I joke, of course. He was very happy in his final years, and he died with a smile on his face in his mistress's bed. I can only hope to be so lucky."

Adrianna wanted to gag, but cleared her throat politely. "So, I hope you enjoy your visit." She let out a small yawn. "I'm really exhausted. As you know, I've been dealing with a crisis."

"I heard, and I'm very sorry," Alesso said.

"You handled it well, *mimma*, I'm so proud of you," Frankie said. "Which means we should celebrate. We're having dinner at *Petite Louve* tonight."

"I didn't get a chance to eat there during my last visit to New York. I only ate at Muccino's of course," Alesso declared.

"Dominic and Aunt Holly said they're preparing a special menu. Your father will be there," Frankie said. "And—"

"Pardon me for the interruption. I just wanted to let Miss Anderson know I've arrived."

Adrianna's heart soared when she heard the familiar voice. "Darius," she said, trying to make her voice as even as possible. "You're here."

"I apologize, Alpha," he said to Frankie. "I was delayed on my way here."

Delayed? He should have arrived yesterday. "I'm glad you're back," Adrianna said, giving him a warm smile.

"Yes, so am I," Frankie said. "Darius, I wanted to thank you personally for saving my daughter's life. I owe you a debt I can never repay."

His jaw tightened. "It was my duty, Alpha, to protect you and yours."

"I've already spoken with your uncle and I assured him that you and your, er, family will be rewarded generously," Frankie said.

"Thank you, Alpha." He bowed his head. "If there is nothing else you need me for ..."

"You may go, of course," Frankie said.

Adrianna watched helplessly as Darius pivoted and left, not even giving her a second glance. She wanted to go after him and ask him how he was. Her wolf too, was elated at the sight of him, and urged her to go after him. But she knew she couldn't be rude to their guest. Besides, she had already decided to tell Frankie about Darius, as it would be better coming from her and not Julianna. But she couldn't exactly do that in front of Alesso.

"So, Adrianna, what do you say?"

"Huh?"

Frankie raised a brow at her. "Dinner?"

She felt a headache coming on. "I'm really tired, Mama."

"But Alesso's only here for tonight," she said.

"If you're tired, Adrianna, I understand," Alesso said. "Disappointed, but I understand, given what you have gone through."

Her mother gave her a pleading look, and Adrianna sighed. "Can you ... give me a second please?" she asked. "I just ... let me er, get refreshed and I'll come down and let you know how I feel."

"Excellent." Frankie clapped her hands together. "We'll be right here."

Adrianna hoped neither Frankie or Alesso noticed how fast she dashed out of the living room. She knew what her mother was up to. After all, it was only days ago she tried to matchmake with William. She was going to put a stop to this, because she wasn't interested in any of the men her mother presented. In fact, she was only interested in one, albeit one who was currently missing.

She took a deep breath and called her wolf, hoping it would pick up Darius's scent. True enough, she got a hint of vanilla in the air and followed it outside to the back porch, where he was standing, his back to her.

"Darius!"

He turned around slowly. "Miss Anderson."

She tried not to flinch at his formality. "I'm sorry, that was awkward." She sucked in a breath. "She just kind of ambushed me, being here and bringing Alesso with her."

"It's *fine*."

She knew it wasn't fine. From the way his entire body stiffened and how his teeth ground together, he was not *fine*. "Darius. We should talk—"

"I must secure the perimeter." He turned away from her. "You never know what could have happened in the last two days. Our defenses may have been breached."

"Darius, don't—"

He didn't seem to hear her, and she watched, her heart sinking all the way to her stomach as he walked away from her. She pushed down the burning at her throat, swallowing the bitterness she felt. If only her mother hadn't shown up with Alesso. She and Darius could have had some time alone, maybe to talk. Instead, now he was probably mad at her, thinking she wanted to go out with Alesso. She could only hope that he would talk to her.

"Adrianna? I thought you went upstairs to get refreshed?"

The sound of her mother's voice made her jump. She took a deep breath and turned around. "Sorry. I was just ... I need some fresh air."

Frankie put an arm around her. "Are you still traumatized by what happened? Just take deep breaths, *mimma*. You don't have to come tonight if you don't want to."

"I don't?"

"Alesso's going to be disappointed. Lucas, too."

"Lucas?" she asked hopefully. "Lucas will be there?"

"Your father approved it, and we're bringing extra security with us. Lucas was pretty insistent on coming, especially if you were going to be there."

It had only been three days since she saw Lucas, but it seemed like it was forever. Maybe seeing her brother would help cheer her up. "Of course I'll be there."

"Wonderful!" Frankie exclaimed. "By the way, I have something special for you from Rome. It's in your room. I hope you'll wear it tonight, I want to see how it looks on you."

"What is it?"

"It's a surprise," her mother said mysteriously.

She wasn't sure she wanted any more of Frankie's "surprises", but she wasn't in the mood to argue. "All right."

"We're going to head out now. I'll tell Alesso the good news. Go ahead and get some rest, *mimma*, no need to say goodbye. We'll see you soon enough." Frankie gave her a kiss on the cheek then left her alone on the porch.

She shivered involuntarily when a cold gust of wind blew by. She rubbed her arms and turned to go back inside but stopped when she heard a long howl in the distance. *Darius*. Her own she-wolf cried out, her ears ringing with the duet of her inner animal and Darius's, singing a doleful song. She wanted him to come back so they could talk. Her mind was a mess, and she would do anything to see him the way he was in the past two days when it was just the two of them. She wanted his arms around her, to reassure her that what they had was real.

She waited and waited, hoping he would come back.

The sun had begun to set in the distance and sadness turned to despair, and somehow, as her mind went in circles, anger seeped in. How could he just leave her like that? Didn't he think what they shared meant a lot to her? Had it meant anything to him?

Annoyed at herself for acting like some lovesick schoolgirl, she stormed inside, letting the door slam loudly behind her. Let him stew in his own juices. If he was going to act like a jerk, she wanted no part of it. He could sulk alone. She was going to take a long luxurious bubble bath, get dressed, see her family, eat delicious French food, and show Darius that things were just *fine* for her, too.

After a long luxurious bubble bath, Adrianna felt calmer and more relaxed. Her wolf, however, was not, but she was getting impatient with the damned thing, so she ignored its whines and cries. She was determined to have a good time tonight, to move on and forget ... whatever it was she and Darius had.

She put on her makeup, some perfume, and some lingerie—because nothing made her feel better than wearing something lacy and sexy under her clothes—then walked over to her closet. She unzipped the garment bag hanging from the hook, carefully taking out the dress and laying it on the bed.

The red, off-the-shoulder dress was truly breathtaking. She gasped out loud and nearly cried when she saw it. Her grandmother Guilia had the exact same vintage Valentino dress that Frankie loved to wear, but over the years it had gotten old and delicate, so she had it preserved and put in storage. Her mother had always talked about buying something similar or having it recreated. And it looked like she finally got around to it, and custom-made at Maison Valentino to boot. She thought there was no way it would fit her—though she and Frankie were both curvy, she was taller. To her surprise it was a perfect fit, down to the length of the hem. Frankie had this dress made just for her.

Her heart was racing as she descended the stairs; why, she didn't know. Was Darius still there? She supposed she was taking it for granted he would be or that he was even going to drive her to dinner. If he wasn't, then it wouldn't be a problem to have someone fetch her. Her damn brain and heart were at war, with the former wanting him out of her life and the latter longing to see him again.

When she heard the familiar sound of the Dodge Charger engine outside, her heart soared and fluttered in her chest. She dashed outside, lifting her skirt so she wouldn't stumble on it. When she stepped out, she saw Darius, standing next to his car, the rear passenger door open. The disappointment crushed her heart.

"Good evening, Miss Anderson."

She stiffened her spine. "Good evening," she managed to say before climbing into the back seat.

The tension inside the car was thick, and the normally forty-five-minute trip felt like a lifetime. As soon as they arrived outside *Petite Louve*, she didn't even bother to wait for him to open the door. She stepped out without a word and walked into the restaurant by herself. When she got in, she saw the familiar figure of the restaurant's owner and head chef.

"Adrianna?" Holly Muccino exclaimed. "You look gorgeous! I love that dress."

She kissed the other woman on the cheek. "Thanks, Aunt Holly. You don't look too bad yourself." An understatement, of course. Despite the deeper lines in the corner of her eyes and around her mouth, Aunt Holly looked just as beautiful as she did when she married Uncle Dante. She remembered the first time she came here as a child, playing with Lucas and Hannah in this very dining room. That seemed like a million years ago, back when everything was simpler.

"You're the last one to arrive," Holly said. "C'mon, we have the private dining room set up."

She followed Aunt Holly toward the back. Originally, *Petite Louve* didn't have a private dining room like Muccino's did, but as its popularity grew, their regular VIPs clamored for it, and so they built one. Holly's partner, Sharice, who also happened to be married to her uncle Enzo, designed it herself. It was made to look like a classic French countryside dining room and it was a hit with all their guests.

"Finally," Grant Anderson said as she entered. "Hello, baby."

"Papa!" She couldn't help herself; it felt like she hadn't seen her father in a long time, even though they danced at

Zac and Astrid's wedding. She hugged him tight, breathing in his familiar, ocean-scented smell. "I missed you."

"Ooh, wow," he chuckled at her exuberant greeting. "I missed you, too, baby."

Normally, she would have bristled at the pet name, but she just laughed. "How are you, old man?"

"Old?" Grant mocked. "Old, eh? Well, maybe I'm not so glad to see you."

"Adrianna," Lucas greeted.

She embraced her brother next. "Nice to see you again," she whispered.

"Same here." She was hoping that things had improved with him, but looking at his face, she realized that wasn't the case. In fact, he seemed worse. More weary and irritated. "By the way," he stepped aside. "This is my date, Barbara Davis."

The tall, stunning blonde beside him gave her a bright smile. "Hello, you must be Adrianna," she said and grabbed her hand. "Nice to meet you. I love that dress."

"Thanks. Er, nice to meet you too, Barbara." With her expensive designer dress, highlights that must have cost a fortune, and perfectly-manicured nails, she didn't look like a police officer. And by her scent—gardenias—she was definitely *not* human. She shot her brother a curious look, but he ignored her and instead, lead Barbara to the table.

"Mimma!" Frankie exclaimed. "I knew that dress would look perfect on you."

"Thanks, Mama, it's beautiful."

"You look exquisite," Alesso said as he offered her a glass of champagne. "I'm so glad you decided to come."

"Thank you." She accepted the champagne, but when she put the glass to her lips and got a whiff of the alcohol, her stomach recoiled. "Er, I think I'm a little queasy from the drive over. Maybe later." She glanced around. "Are Julianna or Isabelle coming?" she asked.

"Julianna's at work," Frankie said, then frowned. "Isabelle is supposed to be here, but she's gone AWOL."

"She probably had a crisis. Like her favorite designer retired or something." She loved her youngest sister, but Isabelle tended to be vapid and spoiled. "I'm starving. Are we going to eat soon?"

"Spoken like a true Italian," Alesso declared heartily.

Holly laughed. "I'll head into the kitchen and let Dominic know we're ready to serve dinner. Everyone, please go ahead and get seated."

The food was exquisite as always, and Aunt Holly and Dominic truly outdid themselves with the special meal they created. It was a fusion of French and Italian food, to celebrate their guest of honor, while still maintaining the classic French cooking they were known for.

Adrianna ate her fill, and while the meal was delicious and she loved being around her family, she just felt miserable. Glancing over at Lucas, he looked just as gloomy despite the efforts of his date to engage him in conversation.

At the end of the meal, Dominic Muccino came out to

serve them dessert—a cross between a cannoli and Mille-feuille—and greet his guests.

"Dinner was amazing, Dom," Frankie said.

"Thanks, Aunt Frankie," he replied. "I'm glad you enjoyed it."

Grant motioned for him to sit down. "Dominic, come and stay for a bit."

"I can't—"

"Dom," Holly said gently. "Just stay for a glass of wine."

He finally relented. "Of course." He took his seat on the empty chair beside his mother and accepted the wine she offered. As he took a sip, he met Adrianna's gaze. He smirked when she gave him a knowing look.

If it wasn't for the mismatched eyes, most people wouldn't think Dominic was a Muccino. With his fair coloring and his long blond hair, he looked nothing like his father. In fact, it was a joke in the family that Aunt Holly had somehow spontaneously given birth to him without any assistance from her husband. Dom was also more reserved and aloof, the total opposite of the boisterous and fiery Gio. *The Ice Man*, she'd heard the whispers of the staff, and she guessed that nickname didn't just come from the cold efficiency he employed to run his kitchen.

"Should we have a toast?" Alesso said, raising his glass.

"Excellent idea," Frankie said.

Adrianna discreetly grabbed her water goblet instead of her untouched wine glass.

"To what?" Grant asked.

"How about," Alesso looked at Adrianna meaningfully, "to new friends and new alliances?" Everyone agreed, then raised and clinked their glasses together.

After the toast, it was obvious things were winding down. The staff was coming in to clear the plates, and finally, Grant stood up declaring that it was late. They filed out of the dining room, heading to the front of the restaurant. Aunt Holly had bid them goodnight as she went back to the kitchen. Frankie and Grant's car was the first to arrive and so they left after a few more quick goodbyes.

"It was lovely to meet you, Adrianna," Alesso said as his limo pulled up to the front. "I do hope this isn't the last time we meet."

"Same here," she said weakly.

"Please, come to Rome anytime. You are most welcome." Alesso kissed her hand again, then bid them goodnight before he stepped into his limo.

"Lucas, darling," Barbara cooed. "Would you mind if I went back in? I need to take a quick trip to the ladies' room."

"Go ahead," Lucas said.

"Don't leave without me!" she jested before she stepped back inside.

"She seems nice," Adrianna said. "Exactly your type."

Lucas's head whipped back to her. "And what's that supposed to mean?"

The arrival of the gray Dodge Charger stopped what would probably have been an awkward conversation. Darius stepped out, but before he could open the door,

Lucas approached him. Adrianna stayed where she was, curious as to what her brother was planning.

"Darius," Lucas called.

"Yes, Alpha?" he asked.

"I heard you saved my sister's life." He offered his hand. "Thank you. If you ever need anything, just ask."

"It was my duty, Alpha." He did take Lucas's hand, then leaned forward and said something in a low voice that Adrianna didn't quite catch. Whatever it was made Lucas freeze and his shoulders stiffen. He nodded at Darius then walked back to Adrianna.

She was itching to ask him what Darius had said but she knew better. "I'm glad I came, if only to see you," she said.

"I'm glad too." He glanced back at the door to the restaurant, as if checking to see if Barbara was coming back, then turned to her. "Are you all right, Adrianna?"

She wanted to open up to him, to tell him what she was keeping in her heart, but it looked like he was having enough trouble himself in that same department. "I'm good," she lied. "You should go in and check on Barbara."

"I suppose I should," he said with a long sigh. "Stay safe."

"You too."

She turned and walked toward the car. As she expected, Darius held the door of the rear passenger seat open. Sweeping past him, she climbed in without any protest.

The drive home was quick, thanks to the late hour. By

the time she got home, the anger she felt toward Darius had simmered down. Frankly, she was tired of the whole thing. If he was going to act this way, then there was nothing she could do about it. She couldn't fight it, couldn't make him want her again no matter how hard she tried.

She didn't say a word when he opened the door, just walked straight into the house. Halfway up the steps, she heard the door slam behind her and she stopped. Her hand trembled on the handrail as she steadied herself, her shoulders slumped, and the tears she had been fighting finally streamed down her cheeks.

"Adrianna."

Her fingers tightened around the handrail and her spine went stiff. She wiped the tears from her face. "Y-yes?" she said as she glanced back at him.

Darius stood at the foot of the stairs, his eyes glowing in the dim light. The soft expression made her heart pitter-patter, and her wolf sang at the familiar presence.

"Adrianna, forgive me." He took one step toward her.

She tried to harden her heart. "For what?"

"For breaking my promise." Another step. And another. "For not being here when I said I would."

She let out a choked gasp, and more tears spilled down. "Darius—"

"And for making you cry." He was only one step below, but he still towered over her. He brushed a finger down her cheek to wipe the wetness away.

She twisted her body to face him. "Darius. Please." As her hands slipped up his chest, he swept her up in his arms, and carried her up the stairs. She pressed her nose to his neck, breathing in his scent like she needed it to survive. He walked her across the hall to her room, then set her down by the foot of the bed.

"You're so beautiful," he whispered, running his hand down her face reverently. "When I saw you today, I thought I would die from wanting you."

"You can have me, Darius," she said. "You can have all of me." She reached behind her back and unzipped her dress, letting the silk pool around her feet.

"Fuck," he rasped. "You've been wearing this all this time?"

She was glad she'd put on her best corset, matching panties, the stockings and garter belt. "Yes."

"You'll wear this only for me now, Adrianna." She shivered when he hooked his fingers under the garters and snapped them against her thighs. "You're mine." He growled softly before claiming her lips in a rough, possessing kiss. It was wild and consuming, but Adrianna matched him, arching her back and wrapping her arms around his neck to pull him closer.

She whimpered when he pulled away but let him push her back so she sat on the bed. He pushed her thighs open and kneeled in front of her. "I want to worship you," he said before he pulled the cups of her corset down, nearly ripping it. She gasped when she felt his warm mouth on her nipples, sending a thrill of desire straight down to her core.

When he was done with her breasts, he moved lower,

spreading her legs wider. He pressed his mouth to the front of her damp panties, making her gasp. His tongue pressed against her, moving in a rhythm that stirred her into a frenzy. She heard the sound of ripping lace and soon her panties were nothing more than scraps he tossed aside.

"Look at me," he said. "Watch me while I taste you."

She looked down, watching his lips and his tongue lick at her. It was obscene and filthy, the way he looked as he feasted on her, but it only turned her on more. He kept glancing up at her too, his eyes burning with desire as he pleasured her. A hand slipped between them and his fingers replaced his mouth. He moved his digits, pressing into her while his tongue lapped at her clit.

"*Ungh!*" She lay back on the bed, closing her eyes as explosive, pure pleasure shot through her, making her body shake uncontrollably. He was relentless, pushing her to the edge for more, coaxing her body to come harder. When he finally stopped, she lay there, her chest heaving as she tried to catch her breath.

He crawled over her, covering her body with soft kisses and nips as he made his way to her lips. His mouth was surprisingly gentle, as if savoring every moment. She could feel his cock, hard and demanding, as it brushed up against her hip.

"Wait," she said against his mouth. "I want to make you feel good too."

"Adrianna ..."

She pushed him onto his back, watching his expression turn from confusion to understanding as he realized what she wanted. Getting on her knees beside him, she wrapped her hand around his erect shaft, giving it a gentle squeeze. Taking a deep breath, she lowered her head to take the bulbous tip in her mouth.

He groaned and shoved his fingers into her hair. He tasted all male and musk, with a hint of his vanilla scent. She bobbed her head up and down, taking more and more of him with each downward motion and using her tongue to massage the underside of his shaft. When the tip hit the back of her throat, she relaxed, trying to accommodate as much of him as she could, and wrapped her hand around the base.

"Adrianna!"

She continued to pleasure him with her mouth. She really wanted to know what he tasted like, but he pulled her off impatiently and rolled her onto her back. "I need you. To be inside you. Now." He nudged her legs open and pressed the tip of his cock against her. When she bucked her hips up, he entered her in one motion.

"*Ohhh.*" Her eyes rolled back from the pleasure of being filled by him. When he started to move, she raked her fingers down his arms, and though he flinched, he continued thrusting into her.

"You know what I want, Adrianna," he whispered. "Come for me. I want to feel your wet little pussy squeeze around me and milk my cock."

"Fuck!" His filthy words were enough trigger her orgasm. The tremor inside her grew, spreading through her body as he continued to pound into her. She closed her eyes and buried her face in his neck, muffling the scream that ripped from her mouth.

She didn't even have a chance to recover from her orgasm when he pulled out and flipped her onto her knees. He hauled her hips up against him. "Mine," he growled as he speared her from behind. "All mine."

"Yes!" She pushed her face into the mattress, trying not to cry out as his cock pumped into her, stroking her in just the right spot to have her body trembling again. His hands gripped her ass, squeezing tight as he fucked her. The sound of their skin slapping was almost obscene, but it drove her wild. She pushed back at him, meeting his thrusts and squeezing him as he slammed into her.

When his hand found its way between her legs and stroked her clit, it sent her over the edge, and her back arched as she let the orgasm blow over her. His movements became irregular, and when he pushed into her one last time, she felt his cock spasm and twitch. He grabbed her by the hair and pulled her up, twisting her head to the side. His mouth fixed on her neck, his teeth grazing at the skin there as he suckled on her flesh, while his thrusts began to slow down.

She moaned when he finally stopped, then withdrew from her, his sticky come coating her thighs. It was a good thing Lycans didn't carry diseases, which is why she didn't ask him to wear a condom, plus their fertility rates were quite low. Except in the cases of True Mates.

Oh dear.

Was it even possible?

She racked her brain, trying to remember how True Mates knew each other. There was no definitive way to tell before that first coupling, which always resulted in a pregnancy.

Madre de dio.

The thought of having a baby with Darius, however, wasn't unpleasant. In fact, she felt a warmth inside her just thinking about it. She glanced down at her stomach and imagined it full and heavy with their child.

"I hope that smile is for me," he said as he kissed the side of her neck.

She glanced up at him. "Maybe."

He pushed her down on the bed, then gathered her into his arms, pressing her back against his chest. "If not, then I will give you more reasons to smile."

"I should hope so," she said, her lips curling up. Dare she tell him what she suspected? Did he know about True Mates?

Of course, there was one more question that had been burning in her mind this entire time: Did he love her? Because, True Mates or not, she was pretty sure she loved him already.

"Now you are frowning," he said. "Give me a few minutes and I promise I will make you forget your troubles."

She sighed and settled back against him. *Tomorrow*, she told herself. There was always tomorrow. For now, she was going to enjoy tonight

CHAPTER NINETEEN

When Darius woke up, it was still dark, but glancing at the clock, he saw it was five o'clock in the morning. Gingerly, he removed Adrianna's arms which had tangled themselves around his torso and got up. As his vision adjusted to the darkness, he found his discarded clothes and put them on, keeping his movements minimal so as not to wake her.

He padded down the stairs and outside, then got into his vehicle. The bakery in town should have just opened. He wanted to surprise Adrianna with fresh pastries for breakfast. Surely, she would be hungry when she woke up. The drive over was quick and he was soon on his way back, a large pink box in his hand.

When he arrived yesterday, he was determined to stay away from her bed until he figured out a way to solve the problem of Anatoli's betrayal. He could at least tell her later that he didn't think it was right to sleep with her when he knew what had happened. It hurt him to act so cold around her, and at some point when he saw her with the other Alpha, he wondered if he even deserved her. She should be with someone like that man—rich, powerful, and able to give her everything she wanted. But, seeing her looking so achingly beautiful and knowing he had caused her to be so sad broke his resolve.

And now that he had Adrianna in his arms again, he wasn't letting go. He would tell her everything and confess his feelings for her. It was a gamble, but this is what he had to work with. To wait any longer would destroy the fragile bond they had now.

When he entered through the back door, he didn't expect to see her in the kitchen, the smell of brewing coffee in the air. Her thick dark hair was piled on top of her head and she wore a white silk robe, her feet left bare.

"You're awake," he said. He lifted his hand to show her the box. "I got breakfast."

"Oh. Thank you." She gave him a weak smile and opened the box.

The less than enthusiastic reception didn't bother him too much. She certainly looked hungry enough, but seemed restrained as she took a tentative bite of a Danish. *Maybe she needed some caffeine.* "Is the coffee ready? Do you want to get ready for work soon?"

She swallowed the pastry and then shook her head. "I'm not going to work today."

"You aren't?"

"No." She dusted her hands together. "I called off. Told them I deserved a day off today. I'm just so ... tired."

He knew what tired her out, of course. "Good," he said. "Then you can spend the day resting in bed. With me."

"I don't think I'll get much resting done," she replied wryly.

They sat down to breakfast, and while he thought maybe she was just tired, he could see the change in her this morning. She was quiet and pensive, chewing each bite of food carefully and pondering every sip of coffee. He knew something was bothering her.

"What's wrong?" he finally asked, unable to keep quiet any longer.

She looked up at him and blinked. "What? Nothing."

He sighed then reached over to take her hand. She let out a sharp yelp when he pulled her out of her chair and settled her in his lap, her legs straddling his. "You cannot hide anything from me, Adrianna." There was a tightness in his chest as he asked, "Do you regret last night?"

Her eyes flew open. "What? No."

The tightness eased. "Good." He searched her eyes. "Then you are having other doubts?"

"I ... yes." She bit her lip. "I'm having doubts about my ... responsibilities in the future. And being able to cope with them."

"Doubts? You?" He had never known a more confident and capable woman. "Adrianna, you were born to lead and be Alpha."

She hesitated again. "No, I wasn't. Not me. Lucas maybe, but me ... I've always had doubts. I do still. It's a lot of pressure, you know? All these expectations of me, to be a good leader and Alpha. What if, after coming from a long line of female Alphas, I'm the one to destroy that legacy? And on top of that, what if I'm not fit to be a m—" She covered her mouth suddenly.

"Not fit to be what?" He tipped her chin up when she looked away.

"I'm ... I'm sorry, I can't ... can we just talk about something else?"

He let out a long sigh. "If that's what you want. But, may I say something?"

"Of course."

Cupping her face in his hands, he looked her straight in the eyes. "Adrianna, how could you still have doubt in yourself? After everything you've been through this week? When you handled that crisis with grace and poise? "

"That's different," she said. "I'm the president of Muccino International. It's my job to respond to disasters like that."

"How is it different from being Alpha?" he asked. "You preside over your employees as you do with your clan, guide them and help them do the right things. You put your employees first, above everything, like you should do with the people who look up to you as Alpha. You showed those workers you care and gave them hope when there was only grief and sadness. If this is not being an Alpha, then I don't know what is."

He had never experienced such a thing, not with Anatoli or even his Grandfather, but deep in his heart, he knew this was what a leader should be.

She was looking at him, her face in shock. "Darius ...."

He didn't want to hear her protests anymore, so he silenced her with a kiss. She relaxed against him, opening her mouth to him. He deepened the kiss and rubbed his hands down her back in a soothing manner. "I know what will make you feel like yourself," he said.

She wiggled on his lap. "Oh, you do, do you?"

He let out a laugh, then picked her up and set her on her feet. "We should go for a run."

"A run?"

Grabbing the belt of her robe, he gave it a tug. "I want to see my *lupoaică,*" he said. "To run with her and be free."

She shrugged her robe off. "Let's go then."

The weather had warmed up overnight and the snow that had fallen in the past days had begun to melt, leaving patches of ice here and there. It still wasn't an ideal time to be out, but their bodies would adjust to the weather.

He let her get ahead of him, discarding his clothing along the way, enjoying the sight of her delicious, naked body as she ran from him. *Go and run,* lupoaică. He would catch her eventually and the thought made him lick his lips with anticipation. When she began to shift, he called on his own wolf, feeling his body elongate and his bones snap into place as silvery fur grew all over his body.

He had let her run, thinking she could get away from him. Her wolf was gorgeous, he had always thought so, since the first time he saw her shift, with its thick brown and white fur, pointy ears, and those mismatched eyes. He would know them anywhere. It was fun, this hunt, and he enjoyed watching her roam and be free. But he was ready to claim her again.

His wolf circled around, listening for the pounding of her paws on the ground, anticipating where she would be headed. He pushed his wolf's body to its limits, leaping over logs and bushes to get ahead of her. There was a movement in the thicket to his right, and when her wolf leapt out, he was ready.

The she-wolf was startled to see him and tried to stop, but it was too late. Its body hurtled into him, and they rolled on the ground. He started shifting back to his human form, forcing her to do the same lest she crush him. When they were both fully human, he landed on his back with her above him.

"You're mine," she said with a grin. "I caught you."

He didn't point out that technically, he had been waiting for her and she collided into him. "You're right, Alpha," he growled. "So, take what you want."

She lifted herself on her knees, grabbing his already hard cock and pointing it to her slick entrance, then impaled herself on him.

His she-wolf was wild and wanton as she sought her pleasure. He watched her, his pleasure building up as she bounced on top of him, her full breasts on display. He reached up to cup them, feeling the weight in his hands.

She was magnificent. Her skin glowed and her hair

shone like polished black marble. She even smelled different, like something in her had changed. Her body shuddered as she clamped around him.

"Adrianna!" he grunted, unable to stop himself as he felt his pleasure coming on. Normally, he would have wanted to have her come at least three times before him, but just this once, he would let himself go.

She fell on top of him, her breath ragged. He kissed the side of her neck, slick with a sheen of sweat. Her scent was strongest there at the pulse, and he nuzzled it, bathing and soaking in it. There was definitely something different about her. But what?

"Thank you," she whispered. "I really needed this." She got to her feet and then helped him up. "Darius?"

"Yes?"

"I ..." She blushed, then wrung her hands together. "I need to tell you something."

"What is it?"

"I ... well ..." A hand went down to cover her belly. "I can't do it when we're naked like this."

Was she nervous? What did she want to tell him? "Whatever you wish. Let's go back into the house and we can talk there."

They had gone farther than he thought, and by the time they neared the house, the sun had already gone down. He found his pants somewhere in the backyard and put them on, then gave her his shirt to wear since she had left her robe in the kitchen.

"Thanks," she said as she slipped the white shirt over her head. "I was starting to get cold."

He hurried her up the porch steps and into the kitchen, eager to find out what it was she wanted to tell him. However, when they walked inside, the house wasn't as empty as they had left it.

"I was wondering where you two had gone," Julianna said. She wasn't by herself, though, there was another woman standing next to her.

"Mika!" Adrianna greeted. "It's nice to see you."

"Hello, Adrianna." The woman's gaze flickered to Darius. The green gaze held his, unflinching.

"What are you doing here?" Adrianna asked.

"So, you're still sleeping with him?" Julianna accused.

Adrianna grabbed his hand. "What am I supposed to do? Give in to you because you threw a tantrum? Grow up, Julianna."

"Me, grow up?"

"Yes! And I can't believe you would drag our cousin into this." She looked at Mika. "I'm so sorry you have to be here."

"Ha!" Julianna sneered. "When Mama finds out—"

"Oh, she definitely will!" Adrianna's voice rose. "I'm going to tell her how you've been acting like a brat. After I tell her about Darius and me."

Her words stunned him. "Adrianna? What do you mean?"

"It's all right, Darius." She gave his hand a reassuring

squeeze. "She needs to know. And you need to know something."

"Stop right there," Julianna bellowed. "Before you say anything else, you need to hear what we came here to say."

"And what is that?" Adrianna asked.

Furious blue and green eyes narrowed at him. "I knew there was something wrong with him. My instinct was screaming that he and his scum uncle were up to something."

"Julianna—"

"That's why I brought Mika," she interrupted. "You probably wouldn't believe me—your own sister—but you'd believe what she had to say."

Darius felt a tick in his jaw. Who was this woman?

"We've been investigating your attempted kidnapping," Mika said. "It's my job, as deputy chief of the Special Investigations unit of the Lycan Security Team."

Adrianna shrugged. "I know. But why are you here? Did you get more information about the mages?"

Mika looked to Julianna, then back at Adrianna. "I did find out more. We tracked down the four men who tried to kidnap you. Although the security cameras had been blacked out, Julianna was able to find the footage of the men who disabled the cameras."

"Using the D.C. police database, we were able positively identify all of them. Each had a rap sheet a mile long. And those four men worked for a construction company. Corvinus Construction."

"See?" Julianna planted her hands on her hips. "I knew

he and his slimy uncle were up to something. They were behind your kidnapping."

"That doesn't prove anything," Adrianna said.

"We tracked them down," Mika said. "Well, three of them anyway. The fourth man had been found dumped by the side of the road, a bullet in his chest."

He felt trapped. Adrianna's hand gripped his tighter, but he already knew where this was going. His entire life was falling apart in front of him, and he was helpless to stop it.

"The three guys were easy to round up," Julianna scoffed. "And they sang like birds once we exerted enough pressure." She took something off the table—a small tablet PC. She turned it toward them and tapped a button.

A face appeared on the screen as it flickered to life. Darius tensed, recognizing it as one of the men he had taken down as he tried to get to Adrianna. His face was bloody and his lip split.

"Who gave you the orders to kidnap the girl?" Came an unknown male voice offscreen.

"I ... it was ... Charlie." He coughed. "It was easy money, he said."

"Who paid you?"

"I don't know, but I followed him when he was getting the first payment. Just in case he decided to double cross us and run," the man said. "I saw them meeting at one of the construction sites we worked at. It was the boss. Corvinus."

"Turn it off!" Adrianna cried. "Now."

"Do you believe me now?" Julianna said.

Adrianna turned to him, an inscrutable look on her face. "Did you know?"

"Of course he did! He—"

"I'm not talking to you," she hissed at her sister. "Did. You. Know."

He couldn't move. There was no way he was going to lie to her, but at the same time, admitting the truth would hurt her. "I swear, Adrianna—"

"Answer yes or no," she said in a deadly, cold voice. "Did you know it was your uncle who ordered the kidnapping?"

"Not right away," he said.

"When did you find out?" Adrianna's gaze bore into him.

"After I came back from D.C."

"After—" Her eyes widened, realizing what that meant. She had already judged him guilty. And it was his damn fault for not being honest. "You ... you still ..." She turned to Julianna and Mika. "Take him away."

The two women lunged at him, but they didn't realize he was ready. Knowing the possible outcomes of this scenario, his muscles had already tightened and prepared for their attack. First, he swatted Julianna aside, sending her crashing into the counter. Adrianna screamed as she ran to her sister.

He was distracted by Adrianna's helpless cries that he didn't see what was coming. He had seriously underestimated this other woman. Mika had grabbed his shoulders, twisted him around, then slammed him on the kitchen table.

"Stay down, motherfucker," she said.

He turned his head around and saw something metallic glinting in her hands. Cuffs. He had to act fast. Hooking his leg around hers, he caught her by surprise as he swept her off her feet, and she landed on the floor with a thud. Immediately, he bolted and made a run for the kitchen door. He only had a few seconds, but that was all he needed.

He let his wolf take over their body, spurring it on to run as fast as it could. Their heart pumped with a furious beat, using every bit of energy they had to get as far away from the house as possible. He didn't even spare a backward glance, no matter how much he wanted to. This was it, the end of the line. For now, he would have to go back to The Family and Uncle Anatoli. His wolf gnashed its teeth in anger.

We have no choice, he told his wolf. *She is no longer our Alpha.*

Growing up in The Family made Darius who he was—tough, unyielding, and resilient. If he weren't any of those things, The Family would have devoured him and spit him out. Getting back to the compound as a wolf was not as difficult as it seemed. It was a long way from Barnsville, but in Lycan form, he was strong and didn't tire easily.

Plus, he knew the highways by heart and at one point, he snuck into the back of a pickup truck that took him most of the way there. He jumped off when the truck blew past the exit, then made his way to the compound. There was a secret entrance in the back that was set low and could only be opened using a hidden foot pedal. Being in their business, it was not unusual for members of The Family to come home in wolf form if they were in a bind and needed to stay covered or make a quick escape.

He supposed he should be grateful instead of feeling resentful that he had somewhere to get back to. But the pain in his chest wouldn't subside, and all he could think of was the look on Adrianna's face when she realized he had betrayed her. It would surely haunt him for the rest of his days.

As he padded into the compound and made his way to his room, he prepared himself for the confrontation with Anatoli. His uncle was still after Adrianna for some reason, but he was going to protect her, even if she hated him. He would do anything to keep her safe, even sacrifice himself. Right now, his life really wasn't worth much without her anyway. But the only way to make sure she stayed alive was to find out what Anatoli was up to, which meant to keep his uncle's trust. No matter what.

He shifted back into human form and grabbed clean clothes from the dresser, then headed out. He nearly ran into a couple of the younger enforcers as they ran past him in a flurry of activity. *What was going on?*

"Darius? You're back?" Alexandru was right behind

the others but skidded to a stop in front of him. "What happened? Wait, never mind, come with me. Anatoli is asking everyone to assemble."

"Why?"

"I don't know." His brows drew into a frown. "Frankly, I don't know half the things your uncle is doing these days." He gestured for Darius to come with him and he fell in step behind the older man.

Strange. Alexandru was his top enforcer and right-hand man. Why would Anatoli keep anything from him? He followed him all the way to Anatoli's office. As soon as he entered, his uncle's face scrunched up in distaste.

"So, the Alpha's daughter sent you packing, huh?" Anatoli spat.

"Next time you outsource, make sure you hire competent men who won't squeal like pigs," he said in disgust. He rubbed the back of his neck and walked toward the front of his uncle's desk. "Those guys you hired were picked up by the New York's Lycan Security Team and they confessed to everything. I barely escaped those bitches."

Anatoli's laugh was amused. "See how fast they turn on you? Just yesterday, Frankie Anderson was practically ready to get on her knees for me with gratitude and now she's set her whore daughters on you. Looks like you're finally seeing things my way."

"What do we do now? Surely the Alpha will send her people after us."

His uncle's eyes gleamed. "We won't let that happen. It's time I tell you both what I've been working on."

"Sir?" Alexandru's brow raised.

Anatoli gestured behind them. "Meet our ally."

Darius felt the skin on the back of his neck prickle. He turned his head and saw a man standing in the doorway, wearing a red robe. Immediately, he recognized the garment as the same one those men who attacked Adrianna at her ball wore.

Realization swept over him. This man was one of them. The mages.

"Where did you come from? I didn't hear the door open." Alexandru asked. "And who are you?"

"My name does not matter." The man had long black hair and pale skin, and his red eyes held no emotion. It was like staring into a dark red tunnel with no end. "What matters is that we have the same enemy. The Lycans of New York and New Jersey."

It took all his strength to keep his wolf at bay, but Darius managed it. It wanted to rip this man apart and devour the pieces for daring to hurt Adrianna. *We will protect her!* The wolf didn't believe him. *But we cannot let them know we are going to warn her.*

The man's red gaze flickered at him briefly, and for a second, he thought the mage had figured out what he was planning. But he turned back to Anatoli without another word. "Are your forces ready?"

"I am gathering them now," he answered. "And your men?"

"We have been ready for a long time."

"What's the plan?" Darius asked.

"We attack New Jersey before midnight," Anatoli revealed. "We take Adrianna Anderson and kill anyone who gets in our way."

"Why so soon?" Alexandru asked. "What's our attack pattern? Who do we leave to secure the compound? What about a retreat plan?"

"Retreat plan?" Anatoli bellowed. "There is no retreat plan. We succeed or we die. All of us."

"How do we even know Frankie Anderson or her daughter will be there?" Darius asked. "Wouldn't they retreat back to New York? Or somewhere safe?" He could only hope this was the case.

"Frankie Anderson is already in New Jersey." Anatoli's lips curled into a cruel smile. "I made sure of it. And her daughter will stay as well."

"How?"

It was the mage who answered. "We have taken care of it. My acolytes have been deployed throughout the territory causing chaos. The Alpha and her heir will stay to protect their people, and they will be too distracted to defend against a direct assault."

His blood froze in his veins. He could only guess what kind of distraction the mages had employed.

"But we must act fast," Anatoli said. "Before they figure out that we are working together." His eyes gleamed. "Soon, we will be rid of those bitches who dare think they control us! And we will rule this territory and do with it as we see fit!"

"And what about New York?" he pointed out. "How

do you plan to escape the wrath of Grant Anderson after you kill his mate?"

"Grant Anderson is of no consequence," Anatoli said.

"We will take care of him," the mage said. "You do your part and deliver Adrianna Anderson, and you will be rewarded with his territory as well."

His stomach was in knots, but he needed to know what they were planning. "Why not kill the bitch too? She is not Alpha yet and useless. She doesn't even want to be Alpha."

Anatoli's face grew red, but before he could answer, the mage spoke. "Young man," he began. "What is your name?"

"Darius. Darius Corvinus."

The mage cocked his head at Anatoli, who suddenly went stiff as a board and quiet as a mouse. Darius swore he saw a bead of sweat trail down his uncle's forehead. "Adrianna Anderson is none of your concern. The Family will be rich beyond your wildest dreams and own two of the biggest Lycan territories in the world. One woman is a small price to pay."

He felt the claws of his wolf shred his insides as it flew into a rage. It was mentally exhausting to restrain it now, and he feared he would lose control any second. "You are right," he said through gritted teeth. "I must prepare for tonight then. Should I go outside with the rest of the enforcers, Alexandru?"

"I will join you shortly," he said. "I must have a word with your uncle."

He nodded, then strode out the door. As soon as he

was far away enough, he turned a corner, let out a pained growl and dropped to his knees. Its claws felt like hooks, digging into him from the inside.

Stop! Stop, I say! He begged his wolf. *No harm will come to her. I swear.*

It didn't seem to believe him.

"I swear," he whispered. "But you must let me do things my way."

That seemed to calm his wolf down, and he let out a long breath as the claws released him, and he was able to breathe again. When the pain lessened, he staggered to his feet and trudged toward the garage. The Family had numerous vehicles for their use in there, and he could steal one and drive to Jersey to warn Adrianna. She was probably still angry at him, but he didn't care. He was going to make her listen.

He crept into the darkened garage, not bothering to turn the lights on as he walked to the cabinet on the other side where all the keys were kept.

"Where are you going?"

Goddamn Remus! He turned around slowly to face the burly enforcer. "I was searching for a tool." Glancing around, he saw a discarded pair of bolt cutters on a table. "Ah, here it is." He waved the tool in Remus's face. "Tell those idiot mechanics that if they don't return the tools to their proper places, I will use these on their balls."

"Whatever you need to fix can wait," Remus said. "Your uncle needs you to assemble and get ready with the other enforcers."

Was Anatoli having him followed? Did he suspect everything was not right? "Of course." He put the bolt cutters down and brushed past the other man. "I'm headed there now." He walked away from Remus, heading toward the direction of the outside courtyard where the enforcers would be waiting.

He turned a corner when he was sure he was out of Remus's sights, pondering his options. *Damn Anatoli.* Curse him and his greed. He was betraying their kind by working with the mages. Did he not realize the depth of his treachery or did he not care?

Save Adrianna. That was the most important thing now. Obviously, there was no chance for him to get away and warn her. He would have to play along for now and convince his uncle that he was on their side. The moment the mages tried to take Adrianna, he would stop them. He would have to stay close to their leader, the man in the red robe.

A deep, unknown sensation ran down his spine as he thought of that man. There was something about him he just couldn't put his finger on. Something ... familiar?

He cursed as a pain jolted behind his eyes, like a hot poker had pierced into his skull. His stomach roiled, and he heaved and hunched over, trying to wait until the feeling passed. He was Lycan, he never got sick, but this ... what was it?

Remember.

He glanced up and looked around him. Remember what?

"Darius!" Alexandru was standing in front of him. "Are you all right?"

"I'm fine," he said through gritted teeth. The pain had been so bad he didn't see the other man approach him.

"You've been gone for over an hour. Anatoli sent me to find you."

"An hour?"

"Yes," Alexandru said. "Remus said he saw you in the garage an hour ago and he saw you head outside."

"I ..." He massaged his temple. How could he have been in pain for an hour and not realize it?

"Darius, are you all right?" There was real concern in the other man's eyes.

"Is everyone assembling?"

"Yes."

Darius did a double-take. Alexandru had a healing cut on his cheek. When he opened his mouth to ask him about it, the look he gave him made him think twice. "All right, let's go."

CHAPTER TWENTY

Even though Adrianna's life was falling apart, there was no time to wallow or be depressed. "Another one?"

Frankie nodded. "The Wilkinsons. They barely made it out of their house when the mages attacked."

Her heart dropped. "Have we secured everyone?"

Julianna looked up from her tablet. "Almost. Only three families haven't checked in. They live in a rural area so we don't know if they received the alerts we sent out."

"Dad's driving out to check on them, but we haven't heard anything," her cousin Mika said. "We can only wait."

After the truth had been exposed and Darius escaped, Mika and Julianna had tried to go after him, but Frankie's arrival had cut their search short. Reports of attacks on members of the clan started pouring in that afternoon and so as Alpha, she rushed back to New Jersey to figure out what was going on.

The first report was of an elderly Lycan couple living in a trailer park in the south. They were at home when two figures in red robes broke in. The wife was able to escape and call for help, but her husband ... he was not so lucky. Then there was a family who lived down by the shore. They were driving home after picking up their son when they were ambushed by a group of men. One of them was wearing a red robe. They were able to defend themselves, thankfully, but both parents had been seriously injured.

More distress calls had poured in. It was obvious the mages were planning something big, but what? Was it just New Jersey or would New York be under attack too? With everything going on, finding Darius and bringing in Anatoli Corvinus would have to wait.

The kitchen of the Barnsville house had become a command center of sorts. Adrianna and Julianna were coordinating the evacuation of their people while Mika had stayed to help liaison with New York. Grant Anderson was sending as much help as they could spare, of course, but Adrianna knew her father had to think about the people under his protection too. If New Jersey was under attack, then it wasn't farfetched that New York could be their next target.

"It's too bad Daric and Cross are still on assignment," Mika said. "We could use some teleporting warlocks right now."

"How about a dragon?" Frankie said as she put down her phone. "I just spoke with Creed. He's on standby. But you know we can't ask him to come unless we're in real trouble."

Having the only dragon shifter in the world on their side was good backup, but he was too destructive and attracted too much attention when he shifted. They could only ask for his help if things really went south. Still, it was nice to know he was just a call away.

"We'll get through this." Julianna gave Adrianna a reassuring look. "I know it."

It seemed as if the shaky truce between her and her younger sister was holding up. She had expected her to be smug about being right about Darius all along, but to her surprise, her sister had seemed sympathetic and even remorseful.

"*Mimma*, are you all right?" Frankie said. "You look terrible. Why don't you take a rest?

"No, Mama," she snapped. "What kind of future Alpha would I be if I took a nap when we're in a crisis?"

"I just thought you should—"

"No." She'd had to tell Frankie the short version of what happened with Darius. There was no hiding it and though she wished things were different, she'd made her decisions and had to live with them. The only good thing about having to deal with this crisis is that she didn't have to think about Darius and his betrayal. Because surely, if she allowed herself to relive the entire thing in her head, she would go crazy. It was bad enough that her she-wolf was crying in grief, seemingly unable to believe that he could betray them.

Mine. Mine.

"No!"

Three pairs of eyes looked at her. She took in a gulp of breath, feeling nauseous. "Sorry, I—" She stood up and ran out of the kitchen, barely making it to the bathroom as she heaved into the toilet. When her stomach was completely empty of its meager contents, she stood up and went to the sink to clean up.

Pull yourself together. Her clan was depending on her. The mages were out for blood, and she had to defend her people. Defend her family. And defend ...

Her hand involuntarily went to her stomach. When she woke up that morning and threw up in the bathroom, she was even more sure about being pregnant. She had been planning to tell Darius that morning, but a bout of self-doubt paralyzed her. Was she ready to be a mom? What about being Alpha? And the company? How could she juggle all of that?

She couldn't bring herself to look in the mirror. *I'm not fit to be Alpha*. Because surely, an Alpha wouldn't have lost her head over a handsome face and a hot body. Darius's betrayal had cut deep in her heart but also tore down what confidence she had. Worse, he had built her up, saying he believed in her and then turned out to be a lying bastard. Surely, if they were True Mates, he wouldn't have done that? How could she know—

Wait.

She was an idiot. There was one other way to find out if she was pregnant with her True Mate's baby. During the attack, Astrid had survived a fireball because she was carrying Zac's child. Pregnant True Mates were indestructible.

Opening the top drawer under the counter, she grabbed the pair of scissors inside. She held it up, pointing the tip at her forearm. A cut would take a few hours to heal completely for a Lycan. But, if she cut herself and it healed instantly, then she was definitely pregnant and Darius was her True Mate. And if she didn't then ...

"Goddammit," she said in a low whisper. Why was this so hard? It wasn't like not finding out would change anything. But if she were truly honest with herself, she didn't know what would disappoint her more—if she was pregnant or if she *wasn't*. "Dammit." Tears were burning in her throat. She hated this whole situation. Hated herself. And hated that despite his treachery, she still loved Darius.

"Adrianna!"

The voice outside the door and the sharp rapping made her cry out, making her hand slip. "Ow! Fucking hell!" The pointed tip of the scissors sliced down her arm and blood poured out of the gash.

The door flew open, and Mika rushed inside. "Adrianna! Are you okay? What happ—" Her cousin's green eyes doubled in size. "You're hurt! What did you do?"

"It's not what—" The flesh on her arm tingled, making

her gasp. She watched in shock as the wound sealed up in seconds.

"Adrianna?" Mika took two steps forward and grabbed her arm. "Did I just see what I think I saw?"

Her lungs squeezed out all the available air in her body and made it difficult to speak. But she didn't have to explain to her cousin what was going on. Mika, of all people, knew what this meant. Her parents, Alynna and Alex Westbrooke were the first True Mate pairing of their time. Indeed, at that point, most Lycans thought True Mates were a myth. Everyone knew the story of how their parents had discovered they were True Mates and how that seemed to send off a chain reaction of True Mate pairings that haven't been seen since.

"You're pregnant," Mika said in awe. "And Darius is—"

"Don't say it," she said woefully. "I can't do this right now. We have more important things to worry about."

"I—" Her cousin's face turned serious. "I understand. What can I do?"

"I just—" A deep sob escaped out of her throat. "I just don't want to feel this way anymore."

When she burst into tears, her cousin opened her arms and she found herself enveloped in a tight, warm hug. Good old dependable Mika. When they were kids, she'd been a sassy troublemaker, but she had turned out to be most responsible and level-headed out of all of the Anderson–Westbrooke cousins. She was everyone's big sister, always ready to help, while still keeping that mischievous side she had when they were younger. Of course, she was more subdued these days, but it was understandable given the tragedy she had experienced less than a year ago.

"It'll be all right, Adrianna," she said, rubbing a hand down her back. "You'll see. Everything will be all right."

"I just don't–"

"Adrianna! Mika!" Julianna halted to a stop outside the bathroom doorway. "You have–what's going on?"

"Adrianna just needed some time to herself," Mika explained. "Don't worry, letting it out helps."

"The pressure was getting to me," Adrianna quickly explained. "I've never dealt with this before. I don't know how Mama and Papa do this."

Julianna's expression faltered. "I'm sorry, Adrianna. This is my fault."

"What?" She searched her sister's face. "What are you talking about?"

"That ... that scumbag! I shouldn't have ... I mean ..." Julianna gulped hard and hot tears fell down her cheek.

"No, no!" Adrianna embraced her sister. "It's okay. I was the stupid one. I should have listened to you."

"I hate that you're hurting like this, Adrianna," Julianna cried. "I would do anything to make this all go away and have things go back to the way they were, before that bastard ruined it all."

"Oh, Julianna–"

"Oh, fuck!" Julianna's expression shifted, and she wiped her cheeks with the back of her hand. "I came up here because Mama asked me to get you."

"Why?" Mika asked.

"They're coming," she said in a quiet voice.

"The mages are here?"

"We don't know who they are, but our security system is picking up a big group coming our way."

"How many?" Mika asked.

"A lot."

There was no time to waste.

"Mama!" Adrianna called as they hurried down the stairs. Frankie was already by the front door, looking out of the side windows. The grave expression on her face made Adrianna's heart stop. "Mama?"

"They're here. Outside." There was a hard glint in her mother's eyes.

Adrianna gently pushed her mother aside so she could see out the window. Her heart sank. She counted at least twenty men—no, Lycans, she could tell by the way her she-wolf bristled—out on their front lawn. In the middle was Anatoli Corvinus. But there was someone else with him. She felt all the blood in her face drain out. "Mama, is that—?"

"Yes," Frankie said through gritted teeth.

"How—no!"

She couldn't stop her mother from opening the door and stepping out onto the porch. She followed Frankie, as did Mika and Julianna.

"Traitor!" Frankie shouted. "Anatoli Corvinus, you will pay for betraying your kind. How could you side with our sworn enemy? The mages mean to destroy every last one of us. Do you think they will spare you for doing their dirty work?"

"You bitch," Anatoli spat. "Too long you've held us underfoot. The Lycan territorial system is broken, made only to benefit those who rule at the top. Unlike you, my family had to work for everything we had, paid for in blood, sweat, and tears. And now I will take what is rightfully ours."

"What do you want?" Frankie's eyes glowed bright. "Do you want me to surrender my territory in exchange for our lives?"

"You should know by now this is not a negotiation." Anatoli smiled cruelly. "You are outnumbered, and you will die."

Adrianna's blood pumped in her veins and her wolf howled with rage. "I will take down as many of your men as I can before I die." She did have an ace up her sleeve—she was indestructible and she could take down Corvinus. However, there was one hitch to this plan—her mother, Julianna, and Mika were *not*. They could still die. She had to think of a way to get to Corvinus first before they got killed.

He turned his gaze on her. "Oh, no, my dear, you're not going to die. Not tonight at least. So, how about we save ourselves some trouble and do it this way: You go with our friend now"—he nodded toward the mage—"and we will make sure the others' deaths will be quick and merciful? Try to fight and I will kill them slowly while you watch."

"Go to hell," she screamed.

He sneered. "Either way, I will win this fight. You are outnumbered, and no help is on the way."

An idea struck her. If she could get close enough to him, she could try to take him down. "Fine," she said. "I'll come with you."

"No!" Frankie cried out. "Adrianna, I forbid you!"

Anatoli laughed. "Finally. I knew you were a smart bitch." Anatoli stalked toward them, deliberately and slowly, probably enjoying watching them squirm.

Frankie held on to her. "Stop, Adrianna," she said. "You are *not* going with them."

"We fight together." Julianna's voice trembled, but she gripped her other hand tight.

She should have told them, but there was no time. "Trust me, I know what I'm doing." She lowered her voice. "Just get out of here as soon they have me." She looked at Mika meaningfully. "Right?"

Her cousin hesitated, but when her expression changed, she seemed to understand. "Right."

"No," Frankie hissed. "You will not sacrifice yourself."

"Come down here now, bitch." Anatoli was at the foot of the porch steps. "Do it before I change my mind and I have your mother ripped up piece by piece while she's still breathing."

She swallowed hard. "I'm coming." She yanked her hands away from her mother and sister's grasp, but they wouldn't let go. "Stop, please, I—"

A loud growl made them all stop, and when she whipped her head around, she saw a flash of silver tackle Anatoli to the ground.

Darius.

CHAPTER TWENTY-ONE

Darius attacked his uncle without hesitation or second thought. He had been standing by the sidelines, waiting for something to happen, but the moment he realized that Adrianna was serious about giving herself up, he had to act. His wolf tore out of him in a fury of teeth and claws and took Anatoli down. He thought he heard a scream—Adrianna maybe? He wasn't sure as his wolf had taken over their body, and it was out for blood.

The old man was surprised by his actions, but he recovered and fought back. As they rolled around the ground, Anatoli used leverage to throw him off, then Remus and Simion came to hold him down. He struggled but to no avail, as the two Lycans used their strength to keep him at bay.

"I knew it!" Anatoli roared. "I knew you had betrayed us for this bitch!" He was spitting and practically foaming at the mouth. "Stupid boy! Why didn't you die along with your father?" He turned to the mage. "It's your fault! Why did you spare him? Why did you kill the rest of his family and leave him alive?"

Blood roared in Darius ears' as a wave of pain tore through his skull. It was intense, a dozen times more painful than this morning's episode. Remus and Simion held him tighter as his body convulsed and his wolf yowled in pain.

And he remembered.

He was sitting in the kitchen, finishing his English homework.

Mama. Tatâ. Thomsin. Elena.

His parents smiled at each other, like they were hiding a secret.

Then everything happened so fast. The door burst open, and Mama screamed in surprise. Two men in red robes came in, their faces shadowed by hoods. Darius was sitting right near the door, so one of the men grabbed him and pulled him to the side.

The second man waved his hand at his father and said some strange words. He froze, his face went pale and so did his hair, then he dropped to the floor. Mama let out a growl and stepped in front of Thomsin as she began to shift, but the man turned to her now. Again, the strange words came out of his mouth and Mama's eyes went wide. She didn't make a sound, but her hair turned pure white and her body went stiff before she fell back with a loud thud.

Darius was lunging for Elena, but the man holding him down was too strong and pushed him to the ground. He heard two cries—Elena and Thomsin—and then silence. Tears poured down his cheeks as he curled up in fright.

"Look at me," the man said.

Slowly, he lifted his head. The man staring down at him pulled his hood down. Long dark hair fell down his pale face and bloody red eyes fixed at him. He heaved and clutched at his chest. "Hold ... still." When he waved his hand and started uttering those strange words. Darius closed his eyes, waiting for death. Pain spread through his skull and he could feel his heart stop. His limbs went stiff and then ...

"You didn't tell me your half brother had a fully-grown child," the mage said.

The mage's voice—now he knew why it was so familiar —jolted him out of the past and flung back to the present.

"Did it matter?" Anatoli said. "You said you would get rid of all of them."

"You creatures are too stupid to understand the subtleties of how magic works, so I'll forgive your insolence for now," the mage spat back. "But now you can finish the job and then I can leave with what I came for."

Darius opened his mouth to speak, but realized he was still in wolf form. *I must know*, he told his wolf. *Give me our body and we will find the truth.*

The wolf relented, and Darius changed back quickly. The shift startled Remus and Simion, who scrambled backwards as his body changed. He tried to get back to his feet, but the two enforcers were on him again, taking one arm each and then pushing him to his knees.

"I remember," Darius gasped. "I remember everything." He looked at the mage. "You killed my family"

"It seemed I underestimated your resistance to my killing spell and my powers had drained from taking the life of your parents and siblings." He smiled. "I remember too. How sweet it was to see them die."

"So, ready for your punishment?" Anatoli said as he came closer.

"You bastard!" Darius hollered. "You're not fit to be leader of The Family."

"Your Grandfather was already weak and dying," Anatoli sneered. "When he passed away, the mantle was passed on to me, fair and square, as they say in America."

"Why did you kill them?" Darius asked. "What did we ever do to you?"

"What did you do to me?" Anatoli fumed. "Your father was going to steal what was mine! When Mother died, Father found the letters she had been hiding for years. Letters from your grandmother telling him that *she* was his True Mate. He immediately sent for your father. And just like that, Demetri became his favorite son. My father hated me because of what my mother had done and he was so grateful to have your father here. Meanwhile, I was the one shunted aside, even though I worked myself to death to help him build The Family and took on his beatings when he needed someone to act as his punching bag."

Darius was stunned. He never knew this. "You didn't have to have them killed."

"Oh, yes I did." Anatoli let out a distasteful sound.

"When I found out that he chose your father to be his heir and not me, I had to do something." His lips spread into a wide grin. "When they," he cocked his head toward the mage, "approached me and said they would help me take over The Family, I knew it was my chance. Watching my father die of heartbreak was the icing on the cake."

"You bastard!" Darius railed.

"Now you will die, nephew," he said mockingly. "Take him away and kill him."

"No!"

Darius turned his head. It was Adrianna. Her mother and sister were holding her back, but she was fighting them with all her might. "Adrianna! Don't!" He couldn't let her get into their hands. There was only one way he could put a stop to this. "Anatoli Corvinus!" he shouted at his uncle. "I challenge you to a death duel."

Anatoli laughed. "There will be no duel, only your death. I said take him away," he barked at Remus and Simion.

"Stop!"

"What the–you!"

Alexandru stepped forward. "You've been challenged to a death duel, Anatoli Corvinus."

"This is preposterous," Anatoli sputtered. "I am the leader of The Family! By the rules of the old ways, it is my right! Our ancestors said only the strongest of us can lead. They'd been killing each other for centuries for the right to rule."

"That is true," Alexandra said. "But death duels are

also the way of our ancestors as well. So, you must accept and fight or concede defeat."

Anatoli let out a strangled cry and his face went red. "Do something," he hissed at the mage.

"This is your mess," the mage scoffed. "You clean it up. I just want what's mine." He turned to Adrianna. "I will take you when this foolishness is over, and once I do, I will drain every last drop of your blood."

"Damn you," Anatoli sputtered.

Alexandru motioned to Remus and Simion. "Let him go."

"Darius!" Adrianna broke free and ran to him. "Darius, please ... don't do this!"

He wiped the tears streaming down her cheeks. "I must."

"But why?"

"To keep you safe," he said. "Please forgive me for—"

"No, don't say it! I should have known you wouldn't ... Darius please I need to tell you something."

He silenced her with his mouth, savoring the kiss like it was his last. "I need to tell you something too."

"What?"

"I love you, Adrianna."

She froze in his arms. "Darius—"

"You can tell me later," he said. "For now, I must do this." *For you. For my family.* Once Anatoli Corvinus was dead, he would kill the mage next. "Please," he said, calling to Julianna. "Take care of your sister."

"Darius!" Even as he untangled her from his arms, she fought him. Julianna soothed her, prying her away.

It pained him to ignore her, but he had to focus. Anatoli may be older, but he would not give up without a fight. Besides, even if he killed Anatoli, there would be the mage to deal with. Who knew what that scoundrel had up his sleeve?

"Ready?" he asked Anatoli.

His uncle had already stripped his clothes. "You fool. I will kill you and enjoy every minute of it." Anatoli began to shift into his wolf—a large, dark gray wolf that matched Darius in size and bulk. He could feel Anatoli's rage and that's what made him so dangerous. He had everything to lose in this fight and victory would mean he could get rid of Darius and gain two major territories.

But, looking at Adrianna, Darius knew he had everything to lose too. He called on his wolf, and he didn't have to wait long. It was ready to duel to the death to protect her.

The two wolves circled each other, sizing up one another. Anatoli made the first move, bounding forward with paws raised. They swiped and clawed at each other, dodging and parrying off attacks.

Darius's wolf let out a growl and advanced, snapping its gigantic jaw. He thought to push him back until he had no place to go. But Anatoli's wolf wouldn't let itself get boxed in. Much to his surprise, it came forward, leaping up to pounce. Claws scratched at his face and blood blinded Darius's vision.

Anatoli took advantage of the momentary weakness and attacked again. This time, it was his uncle who underestimated him. He rolled to the side and Anatoli went splaying to the ground. The dark gray wolf sprang to its feet and faced him, fury evident on its face. Darius knew it was time.

Attack!

Darius's wolf jumped at Anatoli. The gray wolf raised its front legs, but Darius twisted to the side at the last minute and raked his claws down the other wolf's right side, digging in as deep as he could. It let out a yelp of pain, and Darius's wolf held on, feeling the flesh underneath his claws tear open. They sprawled to the ground and broke apart. Anatoli's wolf got up, but Darius was faster and he attacked—going straight for the neck.

The loud gurgling yelp the gray wolf let out was sickening and Darius did not relish the sound of his uncle's death nor the blood gushing into his mouth. In fact, it disgusted him. But it was all worth it, knowing Adrianna was safe.

Darius released Anatoli's neck and limped away. As soon as he transformed, Alexandru came to his side and helped him to his feet.

"By the old ways, Darius Corvinus is our leader now," he declared. "What are your orders?"

"Stand down," he said in between heaving great gasps of air. The shifting and fighting were taking their toll on his body, plus the claw marks down his face were still throbbing. Once his lungs were fully functional, he waved Alexandru away and stood up straight. "The Family will continue under my leadership, but we will be pledged to the Alpha of New Jersey. Anyone who does not agree is free to leave." He looked up at Frankie Anderson, who stood on top of the porch, a stunned look on her face. "We will obey her rules and serve her. Her allies are our allies and"—he looked at the mage, who stood rooted to his spot, seemingly frozen—"her enemies are our enemies."

"Damn you!" the mage thundered. "You will die, Darius Corvinus!" The mage raised his hands and opened his mouth.

The killing spell. He knew those words, remembered them. The pain began to gather in his skull. He fell to his knees, and as he felt the life leaving his body, he heard a long, low growl, followed by a scream.

The pain was subsiding. His head shot up and the mage was on the ground, a large magnificent brown and white wolf on top of him. Its massive maw was attached to the mage's scrawny neck, tearing into the soft flesh. The mage's body convulsed several times before eventually going very still. The wolf released its victim and turned to him, its mismatched green and blue eyes glowing.

"Adrianna." He gasped and reached out to her, extending a hand. The wolf galloped toward him, licking his hand and nuzzling at his neck. As soon as his arms went around her, she was back in human form.

"Darius," she cried. "Oh. God."

"You saved me, Adrianna," he said.

"Of course I did," she exclaimed. "I love you, you damn fool!"

He chuckled and stroked her back. "I love you, too."

They struggled, but leaned on each other as they got to their feet.

"Adrianna!" Julianna cried as she ran to them. "I thought you were ..."

"I'm fine," she said as Julianna embraced her.

"*Mimma!*" Frankie flew to her side. "Oh God, I thought I was going to lose you."

"Mama," she said. "I'm fine. In fact, I'm—" She stopped suddenly. "Can I please ... can we get cleaned up? I don't want their blood on us anymore."

Darius glance down and realized that his jaw and chest were covered with Anatoli's blood, while Adrianna bore matching stains from the mage.

"Go ahead," Frankie said. "I'll take care of things out here."

"Thank you," she said gratefully. She grabbed Darius' hand. "Let's go."

Darius followed her into the house, but stopped when they got to the foot of the steps. "Adrianna, wait."

"No," she insisted. "Please, come upstairs with me?"

She seemed really eager, so he let her lead him to her room and into the bathroom. She pulled the shower curtains aside and stepped into the claw-foot tub, then motioned for him to join her. It was a tight fit, but they managed and she turned on the shower.

"Oh." She let out a satisfied moan as the hot water

poured over them. He had to admit, it was nice to get the stench of blood off him and feel clean.

"I'm sorry about your family." She turned around to face him, then pressed her face to his chest.

"At least I finally know." Somehow there was a part of him that always thought Anatoli had been responsible for their deaths. He just couldn't find any evidence at the time.

She sighed. "I'm glad we can finally be alone."

"There's so much we need to talk about," he said. "About what happened this morning."

"Shhh." A finger stopped his lips. "No need for that. It's done."

"But I should have been honest from the beginning."

"You still saved me from those men," she said. "You didn't know at that time your uncle was responsible right? It's obvious that he's been keeping you in the dark about his involvement with the mages."

"He's kept everyone in the dark. I think deep down he knew it was wrong, but he was in too deep."

"You still sympathize with him," she said quietly.

"He was abusive and cruel, but that was a product of how he was brought up." His Grandfather had been loving to him and his siblings, but Gregor Corvinus couldn't have grown The Family to what it was if he didn't rule with an iron fist.

"But Anatoli was also a murderer," she reminded him. "Don't feel bad for what you did."

"He was still my blood," he said. "I will have to live with what I did."

"I'll be here for you."

"We're clean," he declared as he turned off the shower. "We should head down. Your mother is probably wondering where we are."

"Yes—oh wait!" She snapped her fingers. "I almost forgot why I needed to get you alone."

"You did?"

"Yes." Her eyes seemed to sparkle. "Darius," she took his hand and pressed it to her belly. "I'm pregnant."

He stood there, dumbfounded, wondering if he heard her right. "You're ..."

"Yes," she said, her voice caught in her throat.

"Are you sure? Isn't it too soon? It's only been a few days. Did you take a test yet?"

She nodded. "Yes, I'm sure. Darius, this isn't just any pup. You and I, we're True Mates."

For the second time in a span of five seconds, he was confounded. But deep in his soul, he knew it was true, that she was meant to be his, the other half of his soul. His wolf too, knew it from the beginning. "I love you," he said with growl, before leaning down to devour her mouth. She parted her lips, allowing him to deepen his kiss. When he finally pulled away, she let out an unhappy sigh.

"We should probably go downstairs," he said. "We can't keep hiding up here."

"I suppose," she said. "But I do want to put all this behind us."

He pulled the shower curtain aside and stepped out, then handed her a towel. "You finish getting dressed. I'll be waiting for you downstairs."

"You promise?"

"I swear." Now and forever, he would always keep all his promises to her.

CHAPTER TWENTY-TWO

Just as he said he would, Darius was waiting by the foot of the stairs. His damp, silvery hair looked like it had been carelessly combed back with fingers, and he was dressed in his usual shirt and jeans. The look he gave her as she came down made the butterflies in her stomach flutter.

She still couldn't believe he was here. And that he was her True Mate and he loved her. It seemed like a dream, and she was afraid she would wake up. He reached out a hand to her and as their fingers touched, she felt that familiar buzz of electricity between them.

"I think we have company," he said, cocking his head toward the kitchen.

She heard voices. Familiar voices. "We should go and see what's going on."

The kitchen was abuzz with activity when they walked

in, and she was taken aback as she wasn't expecting so many people there.

"What's going on here?" Her gaze ping-ponged across the room at all the new faces. "Papa?"

Her father's head turned to her and his face lit up when their eyes met. "Adrianna!" He dashed toward her and cupped her face. "Baby, I thought—" He stopped and looked down, staring at her and Darius's linked hands. "Care to explain what's going on?"

"Papa," she said, pulling Darius closer. "This is Darius Corvinus. My True Mate."

"Your—"

"Adrianna!" Frankie exclaimed and practically leapt across the room. "True Mates? You're sure?"

She nodded. "Yes, Mama." She pressed a hand to her stomach. "I'm going to have his pup." When her father let out a strangled cry, she shot him a warning look. "Papa ..."

Grant let out an indignant harrumph. "I know, I know. As I've been reminded a long time ago, these aren't the dark ages." He massaged the bridge of his nose. "I just ... it seems like yesterday I was waiting for you and your brother to be born." He took a deep, long breath before turning to Darius. "So, you're Darius Corvinus. My daughter's mate."

Darius bowed his head. "Alpha. It's an honor to meet you."

"My mate has told me all about you," Grant began. "She told me that you worked for Anatoli."

"I am his—was," he corrected, "his nephew."

"She also told me that you saved my daughter.

Numerous times." He held out his hand. "I'm grateful, thank you."

Darius seemed stunned, but shook the hand Grant offered. "I would do anything for her, Alpha. She is my mate. I love her and the child that grows in her, and I will protect both of them with my life."

Grant flashed Adrianna a pensive smile. "I have no doubt."

"Papa ..." She embraced her father. "I'm glad you're here. But," she looked around. "What are you all doing here?" She counted a total of seven people that hadn't been here earlier. Her father, three members of the Lycan Security Team, Uncle Dante, and to her surprise, Cross Jonasson, the powerful warlock-Lycan hybrid. Anatoli's right-hand man, the older, burly Lycan who had proclaimed Darius as the new leader of The Family, was there too, talking to Frankie.

"We had come to help. I'm still technically part of the New Jersey clan." Uncle Dante scratched his head. "Though, it looks like you didn't need our help, huh?"

Frankie chuckled. "Didn't you think we could handle things? Are you underestimating the women of our family?"

"I learned long ago never to make that mistake," he quipped.

"Adrianna," Cross began. His blue-green eyes bore right into her and she couldn't help but feel like she was pinned to the spot. "Your mother has relayed to me what happened with the mage that attacked you." He turned to

Darius. "I'm sorry for your loss. That magic the mage used on your family is an abomination."

Darius squeezed her hand tight. "My mate has avenged them."

"Did the mage mention anything important?" Cross asked. "Did he say why he wanted to take you and not just kill you?"

Adrianna shivered. "He said that he wanted my blood."

Those blue-green eyes turned stormy. "Then my initial theory was incorrect. They don't want to stop you from ascending to Alpha. They just want you."

"But what do they want with Adrianna?" Frankie asked.

"They want both of them. Adrianna and Lucas. Specifically, their blood."

"What?" Grant asked, incredulous.

"Do you know how a mage is made?" Cross asked, but it was obviously rhetorical. "Through blood magic. Mages are former witches and warlocks who break the laws of nature by killing and using blood to increase their power. And Adrianna and Lucas, as the firstborn children of two powerful Alphas, have potent blood. I believe they mean to use it for some ritual or spell."

"What kind of spell?" Adrianna asked. Her knees felt weak at the thought. That mage really was going to literally drain her dry.

"I don't know, my father and I are still gathering information." His jaw tightened. "But we will find out soon enough."

"That means we have to be more vigilant," Grant said. "Lucas and Adrianna must be protected at all costs."

"I will have to tell my father about these new developments," Cross said. "This is new information, and we can use it to find out what the mages are really planning."

"We have to find out what they're planning and stop them," Adrianna said. "I refuse to be a target."

"I will be by your side," Darius said. "And I will not let anything happen to you."

"I know you won't." She pressed up to his side, taking in his scent. It wrapped around her, comforted her. She knew from now on, she would do everything in her power to stop the mages and protect her mate and her family.

EPILOGUE

It was one of those rare winter mornings when the sky was bright blue and the air crisp and light. There was an almost ethereal, serene beauty to Greenlawn Cemetery, and the gravestones dotting the landscape didn't mar its loveliness, but rather, enhanced it. The drive there was long, but Adrianna knew it was worth it. Despite the fact that it would be a three-hour drive back to Barnsville, she gladly made the trip.

"We are here," Darius declared as they stopped in front of four gravestones grouped together. The markers were simple etched only with names, but obviously well-cared for. Adrianna stepped around carefully and with Darius' help, placed the four bouquets they had been carrying on top of each grave. She also placed a teddy bear on the smallest one.

They stood side-by-side, hands linked together. The silence between them was comfortable, but she knew this couldn't be easy for him. Last night, he had confessed that although he paid someone to maintain the graves, he hadn't been here in years. "What were they like?" she asked with a gentle squeeze of his hand.

The corner of his lips turned up slightly. "To be honest, the memories of my father are unclear, as I hadn't spent a lot of time with him since he had left us. But from his letters that my mother would read to us every night, I knew he loved us very much. Thomsin was a troublemaker, always getting into things he wasn't supposed to. Elena, she ..." He paused. "Elena was a sweet girl. Always smiling and running to me when I came into a room. I would ruffle her hair and pick her up."

"And your mother?"

Now she saw something she rarely saw—a genuine smile. "My mother was very beautiful and strong. She was very traditional, but fierce. She would have loved you."

"Me?" she asked. "I'm hardly traditional."

"She wouldn't think of tanning our hides if we were in the wrong, but if anyone threatened us, she would rain hell on them." He looked at her with those soulful blue eyes. "She fought hard and loved harder."

"Darius ..." She didn't know what to say, so she embraced him, wrapping her arms around his torso and pulling him close. "I'm sorry," she managed to croak through the burning tears in her throat.

"Do not cry, Adrianna," he soothed. "It's all right. I have made peace with their deaths. And now, I'm so proud to have you here to meet them. You have avenged them, my mate. Thank you."

"I never thought I would be able to take a life. I'm still not okay with what I did." She took a deep breath, wiping the wetness on her cheeks on his shirt. "But I would do it over and over again to save you."

They stood there for a few more minutes, not saying anything, just allowing the serenity and peace to blanket them. Finally, Darius pulled away. "Let's go, my mate. You do not want to be late to your own ascension ceremony."

"And we still have to stop by the compound," she reminded him.

"Of course," he said. "We have *business* to take care of."

Upon Anatoli's death, all his interests in Corvinus Construction and Corvinus Trucking automatically went to his closest living relative—Darius. He declared that he didn't have a head for business and was considering selling everything when Adrianna told him to think about it. After all, both companies had grown so much, plus employed many of the Lycans they had brought over from Romania. When she told him that an unscrupulous buyer could strip everything and lay off people, he reconsidered. Plus, there was the matter of turning everything legitimate and undoing and unraveling all of Anatoli's complicated business dealings. He hated the business part of, well, *the business*, but Adrianna offered her expertise and he accepted.

The drive to the compound wasn't too long, and soon they were pulling into the gates. The men who were standing guard at the main entrance immediately stood at attention, then bowed their heads as they passed. Surprisingly, none of Anatoli's men left when Darius took over. It seemed everyone hated how the old man had kept everyone in line with terror and violence, and they were only too glad to be under someone who they at least respected.

They made their way to the main office—Anatoli's old office—and knocked on the door.

"I swear to God, Alexandru, if you're coming here to tell me how to do my job, I'm going to—" Mila's eyes went wide when she saw Darius and Adrianna walk in. She cursed under her breath. "Sorry, I thought you were—" She stood up and smoothed her hair down. "Darius. Primul," she said, with a respectful bow of her head.

"Not yet," Adrianna laughed. "I'm not Alpha yet."

"Tonight, she will be," Darius said. "And how is everything coming along?"

"Good," she said, then frowned. "But I'd get more things done in a day if that ... brute would stay out of my way."

Darius looked like he was suppressing a smile. "I'll speak with Alexandru."

"Thank you," she said. "Now, let me pull up that report for you."

Adrianna had thought for sure Mila would be the one of the first to leave, but to her surprise, the other Lycan not only stayed, but volunteered to help them legitimize The Family's interests.

It turns out, Anatoli had been asking her to do the books these past few years and not only was she organized, but also brilliant with numbers. Adrianna was ashamed that she underestimated the other woman, probably because of the way she acted and dressed, and how she flirted with any attractive young man in her vicinity. Darius also told her how Mila had helped warn him about the men in D.C. Anatoli sent after her. Though it was to save him and not her, Adrianna was nevertheless glad for the intervention.

"This is good," she said as she looked over the pages that Mila had printed. "Really good."

"It's going to take work," Mila said. "But we can untangle everything eventually. I've already started with the projects we have over in Petersville. I should be able to re-do the contract, though the sheriff won't be happy he won't be getting his take every month."

"Leave him to me," Darius said with a deadly edge in his voice.

"Darius!" Adrianna admonished.

"What?" he said. "This is the side of the business I truly understand."

She knew it wouldn't be easy to undo all of the illegal business The Family was into, but with time and work, she knew they could accomplish it. Frankie still agreed that it would be too risky to just shut everything down, as a vacuum of power would only mean that another organization would take The Family's place. And, she vowed that when she was Alpha, she would never let that happen in her territory.

However, she now truly understood why Frankie decided to move her life to New York. Adrianna loved Darius so much, she couldn't bear to be away from him. In the past week, he had to keep running back and forth between Barnsville and the compound, and the nights he spent away from her were torture. They still hadn't decided what their living arrangements would be in the future, especially when the baby came, but she figured they could work it out.

"If that's everything, then we will head back," Darius said.

"For now." Mila turned back to her screen. "But I'll let you know if I find anything else significant."

"Thanks, Mila," she said. "Is there anything I can do for you? To say thank you?"

The other Lycan grinned. "If you could please bring some of your delicious tiramisu when you come back, that would be payment enough."

"Will do."

They said their goodbyes and left the office. When they got outside, Alexandru was waiting for them, several cars lined up behind Darius's Dodge Charger.

"Is everyone ready?" Darius asked.

The enforcer nodded. "Yes."

"Good." Darius surveyed the other vehicles. "Have two vehicles in front of us at all times and the rest behind."

"Cristian has already driven ahead to scout for any danger."

"Is this all really necessary?" Adrianna asked. "We were fine on the way here. You already have two guys tailing us at all times." She was still nervous about having bodyguards following her all the time, but they mostly kept their distance.

"I will not take any chances." Darius's jaw set into a firm, determined line. "Nothing will stop your ascension ceremony tonight."

With Darius by her side, she was sure nothing would go wrong today. "All right, my mate," she said. "I'm in your capable hands. Let's go home."

Darius surveyed the outside as he stood on the front porch of the old Victorian house.

"Everyone is in position," Alexandru said as he climbed the steps. "No one will be able to enter or leave without us knowing it."

"Thank you," he paused, then added, "for everything." There was no need to say the exact words. A silent understanding had passed between them, one that conveyed his gratitude for the older man's support from the beginning.

Alexandru's expression never changed. "I remained silent for so long because a good soldier only takes orders. I was grateful that your grandfather brought me here and gave me a better life, and that loyalty was transferred to your uncle. My only regret is that I didn't speak up when I knew I should have."

"You and me both. But I promise you, my friend, things will be changing." And that was another promise he vowed to keep.

"I look forward to it. Now," Alexandru said. "Is there anything else?"

"No, we are good." As the older man descended the steps, he did think of something. "Wait."

He turned back. "Yes?"

"There is a tray of tiramisu in the fridge."

Alexandru cocked his head. "And?"

"Please bring it back to the compound with you and give it to Mila," he said. "I was told it's her favorite."

His expression changed for a split-second, so fast Darius thought he missed that slight tilting of the corners of his mouth. Alexandru simply gave him a nod and then continued walking down the steps and into the darkness to take his position. Darius felt confident knowing his most trusted enforcer would be guarding the front of the house. They had gone over the security plans many times and had taken many precautions.

With the mages still a threat, Adrianna decided she would have a small ascension ceremony at home, surrounded by her entire family. It would not only be easier to secure, but she said she didn't want a big celebration. So, the Lycan High Council agreed to hold it in New Jersey and to have a simpler ceremony without all the pomp and circumstance.

Satisfied that the outside was secure, he walked back into the warm, inviting, and crowded home. Normally, his wolf would have protested at being surrounded by so many Lycans in such a small space, but as soon as he saw Adrianna standing in the middle of the dining room, his animal calmed. She must have felt his eyes on her, because she stopped talking and turned her head to meet his gaze. The smile she flashed at him made the entire room brighten, bringing a lightness inside him he'd never felt before meeting her.

He made his way to his mate and slid an arm around her waist, his hand spanning her stomach. She leaned into him naturally, not even breaking her conversation with her sisters and cousins as he came up to her. It made his wolf incredibly proud and happy that she was carrying their pup. He would revel in the sight of her belly growing as she nourished their child with her body, and everyone would know she was his.

"And so, what do you think about introducing some new items to the menu this summer?" Adrianna asked Gio.

"Sounds like a good plan," the Lycan chef replied. "We could do a theme around sustainability and order ingredients sourced within 100 miles from us."

Dominic nodded in agreement. "I know of a few farms you could source some cheese from, they're only upstate."

Julianna sighed and rolled her eyes. "How you guys find all this exciting is beyond me. I'm bored to tears." She turned to Darius. "How about we talk about perimeter defense and the best techniques to disable an enemy?"

"Ugh," Adrianna said with feigned exasperation. "I don't know if I prefer the two of you"—she looked at her sister then at him—"fighting like cats and dogs or getting along and talking shop all the time."

After the whole mage episode, he and Julianna were finally able to put their differences aside and realize they actually worked well together. Now, he was actively helping her in training the new recruits for the New Jersey Lycan Security Team.

"Ugh," Isabelle groaned. "When does this thing end? I have places to be."

Darius had only met Isabelle Anderson tonight, so he wasn't sure what to think of the youngest Anderson. She was pretty, closer to Adrianna and Frankie in looks, but she wore far too much cosmetics and fancy clothing in his opinion. Adrianna described her as spoiled and vapid, but that was due to their father's indulgence of her every whim. Not that his mate sounded bitter; he knew she loved all her siblings, each in her own way.

"I'm sorry to inconvenience you, Isabelle," Adrianna said dryly. "I—" Her expression changed when her gaze drifted across the room and her eyes sparkled as they did when she was excited. "Lucas!"

Darius didn't mind that she left his side temporarily, knowing the bond she shared with her twin was different from theirs. Adrianna embraced her brother and spoke a few words to him before dragging him back to their circle.

"You made it!" Gio exclaimed.

"Of course," Lucas said. "I wouldn't miss this for the

world." He gave his sister a smile, then looked at Darius. "Hello, Darius. I'm glad to see you."

He nodded in deference to Lucas. "I also would not miss this for the world."

"I'm sorry I wasn't there when the mage came here. Thank you by the way," Lucas added. "It seems I'm always thanking you for saving my sister's life."

"There is no need for thanks," he said. "She is my mate and thus I would do anything to keep her safe."

"You're looking chipper, Lucas," Julianna noted. "Glad to see you not brooding so much tonight."

"Maybe it has something to do with that gorgeous brunette he had dinner with at the restaurant the other night," Gio quipped.

"Brunette?" Adrianna, Julianna, and Isabelle exclaimed at the same time.

Lucas shot his cousin a murderous look.

"Don't worry." Gio put his hands up. "I told you, your secret's safe with me."

"It's not much of a secret if you tell everyone that there is one." Lucas massaged his temples with his fingers.

"Are you okay, Lucas?" Adrianna asked. "What are you thinking about?"

"That I should have gone to *Petite Louve* instead," he retorted, glaring at Gio and earning him a rare laugh from Dominic.

"Tell us about this brunette!" Julianna exclaimed. "Who is she? Is she from New York or another clan?"

"Excuse me." Frankie walked over to them, interrupting them. "The Lycan High Council has arrived. We're ready to start."

"Don't think you're getting away with not telling me all about her," Adrianna whispered to her twin.

Lucas sighed. "I know."

Darius sensed the other man's exasperation, so he put a hand on her lower back. "Come, my mate. It's time."

Adrianna narrowed her eyes at her brother, then at him. "What's going on?"

"Nothing." He steered her away from the group. "I'm eager to get this done.

"What did you tell him?"

"Tell him?"

"Lucas." She stopped and faced him, then put her hands on her hips. "That night. After the dinner with Alesso. You said something to Lucas before he left to go back and check on his date. What was it?"

He was trying to be discreet about telling Lucas what happened that night he waited for Adrianna outside the restaurant. At that time, he had thought she hated him so much—or that she was infatuated with the Alpha of Rome —that she wasn't paying attention to him at all. But it seems she had noticed the exchange. "Maybe I will tell you later," he said.

"Later, I'll be your Alpha," she pointed out. "And you *will* tell me."

Grabbing her by the waist, he pulled her to him and nuzzled at her neck. "We will see." He gave the soft skin behind her ear a nip that made her shiver. "You have to promise to be a good girl—Alpha and do as I say when I've got you under me."

"That's not how it works," she said in a breathy voice.

He laughed and sunk his teeth into the place where her shoulder met her neck. That had her moaning and the scent of her arousal tickled his nostrils. His cock surged, and he groaned when it brushed up against her hip.

"Ahem." Grant Anderson was standing in the doorway, his furious green eyes throwing daggers him. "If you lovebirds don't mind, we'd like to get this started."

As his excitement deflated, he bowed his head to the Alpha of New York. "Of course, Alpha." As they passed Adrianna's father, he was muttering something under his breath about "my baby girl", "out of wedlock", and "I hope he has a daughter." Secretly, he smiled. Hopefully, Grant Anderson's worries would be put at ease later on when he planned to talk privately to him and show him the velvet box in his pocket.

Adrianna wanted to have the ceremony in the main living room. This is where she had the happiest times of her life growing up, she had said. It was where her family celebrated every major holiday and most occasions. A few nights ago, she had told him about her great-great-aunt Gianna, and that this was where they had her last birthday before she passed.

All her family was present for this momentous occasion. Aside from her parents and siblings, her uncle Dante and his family, her human half-uncles Enzo, Matt, Rafe, and their families were there. Mika was also in attendance, along with her parents, brothers, and sister. Their paternal grandmother had flown in from Paris and her mother's father, a quiet, older Lycan named Noah was observing in the back. And, since she wanted to feel like everyone was here, there were three portraits sitting on the mantle—two older women whom she explained was her great-grandmother Guilia, and grandmother Adrianna, whom she was named after, and of course, her beloved Nonna Gianna.

"Are we ready?" Sergios Anastos, the head of the Lycan High Council asked. He was standing by the mantle and the four other members were standing behind him. One of them was holding a large, mother-of-pearl inlaid box.

"Yes," Frankie said as she gestured for Adrianna to come stand next to her.

Adrianna took a deep breath and grabbed his hand, tugging him forward. He was surprised that she had asked him to stand to her right, as this was the place reserved for an Alpha's significant other during official events. But he would have gladly stood anywhere—behind her, with everyone else, or even in the back of the room, as long as he was here to witness her ascension. He didn't need a special place of honor, as he would still be her mate no matter what.

"Francesca Anderson," Anastos began. "Do you relinquish your position as Alpha of New Jersey freely and of your own will?"

"I do," Frankie said. "And I nominate my daughter, Adrianna Callista Anderson as my successor."

Anastos turned to Adrianna. "And you accept, Adrianna Callista Anderson?"

"I accept," she replied.

He turned to the council members behind him and gestured toward the woman carrying the ornate box. She opened it, and he reached inside, withdrawing a long, sharp dagger. It was longer than any dagger he'd ever seen, but not quite as long as a sword. The pommel was flat and circular and had a large green gem in the center.

"Adrianna Callista Anderson, the position of Alpha requires many things. Responsibility, loyalty, and an unwavering commitment to protect your clan. Do you vow to protect your territory and those under your care?"

"I do."

"And do you vow to protect our kind?"

"I do."

"And do you vow to abide by our laws and never reveal our true nature to anyone who may harm us?"

"I do." Her voice was strong and steadfast as she answered each question, like the beating of her heart.

Anastos lifted the blade in his hand and turned the tip toward the ceiling. "To show your commitment to the position, you must make your vow with blood."

Though he had already been briefed about the next part of the ceremony, Darius's stomach clenched. However, he stifled the urge to take her hand. This was something she had to do on her own.

Adrianna raised her right hand and then grasped the blade. As her fist squeezed, blood began to flow down the shiny edge of the dagger. The thick, dark liquid dripped down toward the hilt and when a drop hit the jewel, he swore he saw the facets shimmer and change color. Blue. Yellow. Then red. He blinked. *Must have been my imagination.* The green jewel remained as it was.

He turned his attention back to his mate. She didn't make a sound nor did her expression change, and Darius felt a surge of pride in him. She was Alpha. His Alpha.

"The vow has been spoken and sealed with your blood." The serious expression on Anastos's face changed into a wide smile. "Congratulations." He bowed his head low. "Alpha."

The hushed silence in the room was broken by cheers. Adrianna's shoulders relaxed and before she could say anything, Frankie enveloped her in a hug. "I'm so proud of you, *mimma.* You'll be a great Alpha."

"Thank you, Mama." She turned to Darius, but before he could say anything, she was surrounded by her exuberant and lively family members, all seemingly in a competition to get to her first.

"Congratulations, Primul!" Gio exclaimed as he lifted her up and spun her around.

"Hey!" she laughed. "I don't think this is how you're supposed to treat your Alpha." When he put her down, she let him kiss her on the cheek.

"I know you'll do great," her father said as he embraced her.

"Thank you, Papa."

"Well, you now outrank me." Lucas's face, however, was shining with pride.

"I think I've established from the beginning that I've always been the boss," she shot back but wrapped her arms around him when he stepped forward for a hug.

"*Bossy*," he corrected, then stood back and ruffled her hair.

Darius backed away as more family came forward to congratulate her. He didn't mind at all, wanting her to bask in their love and joy. This way, she could feel what he knew all along: that she was going to be an amazing Alpha.

"C'mon, the food's getting cold." Gio waved his hands in the air dramatically. "Dom and I worked hard all day making sure everything was perfect."

"Well, at least we all know where the men in this family belong," Julianna chuckled. "In the kitchen."

As everyone laughed and joked and filed out of the living room, Adrianna went against the crushing tide of bodies—and headed straight for him. He bowed his head low, but before he could say anything, she put a hand up to his lips.

"Don't you dare call me Primul." But she said the words with mirth in her tone.

"I wouldn't dare."

"Good. What would you call me then?"

The words came out with ease. "Mine."

She reached up and pulled him down for a kiss. The touch of her lips warmed all the cold places inside him, as if she was reaching inside to banish the darkness from his soul. And though he had claimed his Alpha, he knew that she too, now owned his heart, body, and his soul.

I hope you enjoyed Adrianna and Darius's story.

I have some extra HOT bonus scenes for you - just join my newsletter here to get access:

http://aliciamontgomeryauthor.com/mailing-list/

You'll get access to ALL the bonus materials from all my books and my **FREE** novella **The Last Blackstone Dragon.**

ABOUT THE AUTHOR

Alicia Montgomery has always dreamed of becoming a romance novel writer. She started writing down her stories in now long-forgotten diaries and notebooks, never thinking that her dream would come true. After taking the well-worn path to a stable career, she is now plunging into the world of self-publishing.

facebook.com/aliciamontgomeryauthor
twitter.com/amontromance
bookbub.com/authors/alicia-montgomery

Printed in the USA
CPSIA information can be obtained
at www.ICGtesting.com
LVHW090355151023
761121LV00001BA/209